Good
Stones

Anne Merrick Epstein

Illustrated by Susan Meddaugh

1977

HOUGHTON MIFFLIN COMPANY BOSTON

Acknowledgments

The writer is indebted to folklorists Stansbury Hagar, Charles G. Leland, and Frank G. Speck. Their work yielded much information on Penobscot ways of life and legends alluded to or retold in these pages.

Grateful acknowledgment is given for permission granted by the University of Pennsylvania Press to reprint Penobscot music and lyrics from *Penobscot Man*, by Frank G. Speck.

Library of Congress Cataloging in Publication Data

Epstein, Anne Merrick.
  Good stones.

  SUMMARY: An aging ex-con who lives as a hermit joins with a twelve-year-old, half-breed orphan and together they make a life for themselves surviving the elements and the rejections of society.
  [1. Abnaki Indians — Fiction. 2. Indians of North America — Fiction. 3. Survival — Fiction. 4. Friendship — Fiction] I. Meddaugh, Susan. II. Title.
PZ7.E72515Go   [Fic]   77-23188
ISBN 0-395-25154-0

To David

Side by side on a high island off the coast of Maine lie two round, honey-colored stones. They look down on a cove whose cold waters move in and out to sea.

The land around the cove is moorlike: in spring it is covered with low-bush blueberries and bracken fern; in fall with the purple haze of wild flax.

Visitors are rare at this lonely spot, except for the regular appearance of a tall Indian woman. She always moves directly to the two stones, as if that is her only purpose in coming. She will sit next to them, pulling her long cotton skirt around her. But first she seems to greet them by bending down, almost embracing the stones with her body.

Her mouth moves. To whom could she be talking out here at the edge of the western hemisphere?

Before she leaves she may touch the stones again. As she moves slowly away toward the forested interior of the island, her face wears a serene expression. She has just done something that enriches her life.

1

I

The summer morning was still; the smallest leaves on the elm tree did not move. A solitary jay perched himself at the end of a branch, surveying a farmhouse below. The house, white and shuttered, sat alone on a hill; beneath it a patchwork of woods and fields surrounded a small village in the valley floor. Mountain spines stretched beyond, edging the horizon with green-black slopes. A New England scene, some forty-odd years ago.

The jay flew off when the back door opened, and a young Indian girl slipped outside. She paused for a moment and took a deep breath, trying to drink in the moist air, which was thick with smells of seed and flower, grass and soil — the wine of midsummer. Moving quickly, she stepped off the back porch and darted into a grove of maple trees. Usually she went directly to the road across the sloping front lawn, but this morning she was afraid of being seen, and so she made a zigzag path down to the road through the maple grove — hidden, she hoped, from a chance gaze through the curtain of a second-floor window.

As she left the shade of the trees and crossed to an open field, sunlight hit her body, revealing that she belonged to the natural world as much as the tawny meadow grass that surrounded her. Her thin, strong body seemed to give off a warm glow of its own, and her progress through the grass was as unconsciously lithe and unwasteful of motion as a wild animal's.

Her face was an Indian face, except for her nose, which was crooked, a hastily thrown-up ridge between the broad planes of her cheeks. Her eyes were big, dark, and bright; her mouth wide and strong. Her chin and jaw were also strong, but her body was surprisingly thin, really too small for her head, so that despite her natural grace she looked a little odd. Behind her back, people called her pumpkin head.

She was alone now. Her mother had died the month before, and as long as she could remember, she'd never had a father. But she was used to being

3

alone — or if not alone, cut off from people. Even while her mother was living, the two of them had felt separate from the small New Hampshire village that was their only contact with the world.

Now and then people in the village used to catch glimpses of them. The mother was gaunt and slightly bent; her dark-haired daughter, moving silently at her side, always wore a faded cotton dress whose looseness accentuated how thin her arms and legs were. They were thought of — whenever anybody bothered to think of them — as two strangers from another world.

It was easiest to assume they wanted to be left alone, and so they were. If anyone passed them as they walked side by side down the twisting road to the general store, the mother might incline her head an inch while the girl studied her worn-out sneakers. A murmur might be exchanged; no more.

No one except Mr. Finch, the store owner, had ever spoken with them, and even he, who loved nothing better than an exchange of friendly banter with his customers, had found it hard to know what to say to the Indian woman. As for the girl, he could only remember her standing, mute, in the darkest corner of the store, over by the radio near the laundry soap. She would stare at him with big eyes, as if she'd never seen such a thing as a bespectacled man wearing a blue sweater.

It was always a relief to Mr. Finch when they slipped out the door. He thought they had queer, other-world ways about them. The mother's eyes would dart over every item on the shelves. When other customers walked in, she'd signal her daughter, they'd get their groceries and pay for them, then leave as fast as they could. The way Mr. Finch saw it, such strangers might as well have come from the sun or the moon, or maybe from some dark mythical underworld he half-remembered reading about when he was a boy.

When the woman died nobody'd given it much thought. People like that were at the edge of the landscape — they were rarely the topic of gossip between neighboring houses. An Indian woman and her daughter had drifted in to work at the Osborns' some years ago; the mother had died; and that was that. As for the girl, people supposed the Osborns were keeping her to help around the house. No one saw her very often.

The Osborns themselves were thought of as oddities. There were just two of them, brother and sister, in the big house out on the hill. People said it was a crime the way Walter Osborn left his spinster sister to manage as best she could while he went off on his drunken sprees, especially now that she had only the Indian girl to help.

There used to be a younger brother, Len, but he'd died in an accident at a lumber camp in Maine. Once in a while a few old-timers might refer to some connection between the two Indians and Len Osborn, but it was a stale story by now.

Not until Sisul had escaped from the house did she

begin to think about where to go. She'd never learned to think ordered thoughts — one, two, three; B follows from A; C from B. It was easier to move through days reacting to whatever happened from moment to moment. When she was hungry, she ate. When she was angry, she cried and hit out. Right now she was running away from the Osborns because it was more unpleasant to stay than to leave.

Yesterday Miss Osborn, Walter's sister, had told Sisul to clean up her brother's room. That meant Walter would be returning today or the next day. Sisul had lain awake most of the night, wondering what new torments lay in store for her on this visit.

Two weeks before, Walter had burst drunkenly into the house and demanded to know where the money was hidden — a crazy demand, since she was sure there was no such thing as hidden money. Even if there were, she, Sisul, would have been the last one to know about it. When she said she didn't know what he was talking about, he twisted her arm behind her back and punched her in the stomach. She should have known better than to kick him. That only provoked him to hit her face with his fist and pull her hair.

It was hard not to scream; she knew that screaming would bring the sister — always known as *Miss* Osborn — who would then blame Sisul for everything and abuse her for days afterward.

Suddenly Walter's mood had changed. He'd started laughing, and then let go of her hair. "You're not such a bad kid," he said, and laughed some more.

Enraged, Sisul had watched him amble out to the kitchen. He lightly touched the faded red flowers on the wallpaper with his finger as he went, as if he were trying to coax her attention away from his former violence.

Upstairs in her room, Sisul had thrown herself on her bed and pounded the mattress with her fists. She couldn't understand why he behaved this way so often. Not only was she angry; she was afraid, too. How often had she watched him hit and punch and torment her mother. When Sisul was younger, her mother had been able to fight back, but as her mother had grown weaker, there'd been nothing to stop him. If Sisul ever tried to interfere, her mother would yell at her, "Go away. Get out of here."

"I'm almost twelve now, Mother. Let me help you!" Sisul would shout back. Her words always went unanswered.

When Sisul went to her mother's room after Walter had left the house, her mother would simply smile weakly and close her eyes, signaling that she was too exhausted to discuss the matter.

Finally, last night, listening fearfully in bed for the sounds of Walter's car on the driveway, it occurred to Sisul that she could run away. Nothing was keeping her in this house now that her mother was dead. She had only to get far enough away so that Walter could never find her.

Now, having slipped noiselessly away from the Osborn property, she pushed through the wet hay of the field on the other side of the road, seeds clinging to

7

her dress and long hair. She passed her free hand over her head — she carried a blanket and a basket in the other — and caught some of the seeds in it. She licked her palm, squeezing her eyes shut, and chewed the seeds, salty with sweat.

It seemed to her that everything worth knowing, including this way of eating seeds, had been learned from her mother. Her mother, Awatawessu, had told her they were Wabanaki Indians — she always said it with stern pride — who'd left their ancestral home in Maine years before and come to work in this New Hampshire town. That was almost all Sisul knew about herself. Exactly why they had left Maine and what reasons had brought them to this place were subjects Awatawessu never discussed. Sisul tried to answer these questions herself, but without success. She only knew that the answers had to lie in the origins of the man who had been her father.

What she did know was that somewhere in an uncertain past there was a place called Wachussami, where she and her mother belonged, a place of dark forests and shining water. However separated they were from that past here in this New Hampshire village, it was still the past that mattered. Her mother led her to believe that what went on around them in their present life was of no importance. It was almost as if they weren't really living here, but were hovering above, looking down on life from some secret place that no one could touch.

Awatawessu never talked with her daughter about what kinds of lives were lived in the clustered white houses of the village, perhaps because she herself didn't know. What instincts pushed the people who lived there, what mysteries and dreams lay unfolding behind thick winterproof doors, remained unknown to Sisul — unguessable, even. Mr. Finch was right: they were wanderers from another world.

But her mother taught Sisul what she considered important, and did so with a vengeance. The things Awatawessu had learned as a child, reared in the small Indian village in the north — to know, until it was instinct, the meanings of nature's flickering lights and shadows; to read the signals of earth and sky; to believe that a spirit dwelled in everything — those were the important things.

"Even the stones have a voice," Awatawessu would say, and to demonstrate, she would pick up a rock, run her hands over it, and hold it to her ear.

"This one is round," she would explain. "It fell down from the mountains; someone was angry. Maybe Gluskabe threw it down."

The hand of Gluskabe, the godlike hero of Wabanaki myth, touched everything — earth, trees, rivers, the sea and stars, and the smallest pebble. He had given animals their present shapes, and named them; he had created Indian people out of the bark of ash trees. He was responsible for seasons, for wind and snow, for ocean tides. Wabanaki stories of creation and conflict lived in every natural thing, and their telling and retelling made Sisul feel there was a thread vibrating between herself and the world. If she had known about electric currents, she might have imagined a line of dancing electrons leading from leaves, stones, water — everything she touched — to her hand.

But Sisul hadn't gone to school. She had never learned to read. She could tell you where in the fields the *penapsk*, a kind of wild potato, grew best, and she could tell you the "moons" of the year by observing the positions of certain stars, but she couldn't add or subtract beyond the fingers on her hands.

Neither had she learned how to behave when anyone outside the immediate circle of her mother and the Osborns spoke to her. Fortunately it had occurred only once or twice, since she was terrified when it happened.

"What's your name?" a girl with a new Dutch haircut asked her once.

"Sisul," she whispered into the ground. The girl had an odd look on her face, Sisul thought, and she was sure she was being laughed at.

"What did you say?" the girl insisted. "I couldn't hear you." "SEE-sul," she threw out fiercely; then ran off home. Catching sight of the back of a Dutch haircut again one day, Sisul quickly moved away before there was time for the girl to notice her.

It was a problem, and she was tormented by it. She was being raised as if the world of schools and townspeople and girls with stylish haircuts didn't matter. Yet this world surrounded her; it could easily swallow her up. How was she to keep away from it? How could she block it out, especially when that other world — the Wabanaki world — was so distant, really little more than a dark memory?

And so she began to live a double life inside her head. She pretended to be proud, truckling to no one. She was a Wabanaki! But secretly she knew how weak she could be. How many hours had she spent daydreaming about the lives of girls with blond hair who wore pink dresses and ambled down the road as if the world belonged to them? How often had she stood in Finch's store, listening to people pass the time of day; then later worked the conversations over in her mind, saying to herself, this is how *real* people act and laugh?

Sometimes she would pretend to be some of those people, talking avidly to herself about the weather, about her children: "That Johnny's the limit! Do you know what he did yesterday, Mr. Finch? Why, he took my clothesline down and made it into a lasso and he's been rounding up cows all day, just like he saw at the pictures." Laughter. Shaking of heads. Then — but Sisul left out this part — the usual uneasy glance was cast in the Indian woman's direction.

Sisul was ashamed of these moments in her life — it was weak to want to be like these people, she told herself. Angrily she pushed her daydreams away. But she knew they lurked down there where her secret thoughts lay; she could feel them accumulating like so much hidden trash.

She stopped to catch her breath and paused for a moment in the field, turning her face toward the village. It beckoned, a pretty miniature lying at the bottom of the hill. Within those neat frame houses lay things she had never seen and could hardly imagine. Now that she was free to do as she wanted, why not go toward it? Maybe someone there would feel sorry for her and take her in.

Ah, there it was, the old weakness again! A feeling of disgust washed over her, along with a determination to be steadfast to the life her mother had wanted for her. At that moment, standing alone in the field in the early morning, she promised herself she would never, never give in to softness or ease, and that she would never, never bend to the will of anyone, no matter what the rewards. Only in that way could she be true to her mother.

She couldn't remember that Awatawessu had ever put such ideas into actual words. She hadn't needed to; they were given off like breath from her pores. Awatawessu's every look and gesture spoke defiance and ramrod strength. Even through the weeks of increasing weakness before her death, her eyes had fought back, and Sisul felt as if she always heard a voice whispering, "You must never give in; you must never give in."

The sun was well above the mountains now. Dark strawberries were ripe between the stalks of field grass. Occasionally Sisul allowed herself to stoop and pick one, but since she had made up her mind about where to go, she was in a hurry to get to the muddy, slow-moving creek that bordered the field.

It was a favorite swimming place. No one was there so early in the morning; mist still rose off the surface. Locusts had set up a hum, signaling sun and heat — it would feel good to slip her naked body into the soupy water and quietly paddle around.

At the last minute she changed her mind, afraid of losing time or of being seen, and instead she turned left, away from the maples swaying over the brown water.

Farther upstream the creek narrowed and became shallow enough to wade across. A stream ran lazily through the field that lay on the other side, its source far up on the mountain, where it rushed across glistening rocks. As if this had been her plan all along, she suddenly knew that she must follow the stream up the mountain. It would be a pathway taking her farther and farther away from the dead, airless rooms of the house she had crept from, and from the village that grew smaller and less important with each step she took.

II

By midafternoon Sisul hadn't found a place to stop,
but she had gotten far enough away to feel safe. It
wouldn't be easy for anyone to find her in such thick
dark woods, she thought. After walking for almost
eight hours, never straying far from the stream's side,
she was about halfway up the mountain.

"Eat half if you want; put the rest in your basket,"
ran through her mind, as if her mother were next to
her, whispering in her ear while she stripped berries

and pulled up *penapsks* on her way. She stuck to the rule, except for some velvety raspberries that would only be squashed, she told herself, if she tried to save them.

Her eye fell on a flat rock up ahead, sloping under a tall bull pine. She was tired. This would be as good a place as any to squat down and have a meal. The *penapsks* were barely edible uncooked, but a fire would be foolhardy. If people were on the lookout, a thin column of smoke rising off the mountain would lead them right to her.

Sitting on the rock with her knees up to her chin, reaching back and forth into her basket for food, she felt a sense of peace float down upon her like a silent descent of leaves from the trees that wove shadows above her head. Since Awatawessu's death, Sisul had asked herself over and over again what her mother would have wanted her to do. She sensed that her mother had wanted to say, "Go back to Wachussami." But the words had never actually been spoken. "Always remember everything I have told you," was all she ever said in that once-strong voice that by the end had sunk to a bare whisper.

Sisul thought now of going to Wachussami. Where was it? Maine, up north, was all she knew. But if she left this mountainside and started to walk there, somebody would be sure to notice a twelve-year-old girl out on the road by herself. She'd be picked up and brought back to the Osborns. No, she thought, she mustn't let herself be seen by anyone, not for a very long time. But what should she do?

Effortlessly, by themselves, plans seemed to spin out in her mind. She had gotten herself away from the house and partway up the mountain. That much was done, accomplished. Now the question was whether she could stay up here, or near here. Why not? It was peaceful, there was food available, water ... the only thing left to find was shelter, and that shouldn't be hard. She liked it here on this mountain. She had no doubts about taking care of herself. Hadn't her mother taught her everything she needed to know?

Sisul thought back to long afternoons spent in meadows and woods, and it was suddenly plain to her that for over a year her mother had been preparing her to live just this way.

She could almost hear the serious tone of Awatawessu's voice as she recalled kneeling with her under a hot sky, picking Juneberries. "Most food keeps through winter if you dry it first," her mother had said. "You must spread berries and roots on a rock in the sun and keep turning them. They get dry, like seeds." Then Awatawessu had glanced over to make sure that her daughter was paying attention. "The sun does it," she'd added sternly. "Don't let them sit out in damp air."

That spring a whole week of afternoons stolen away from the Osborns had been devoted to making storage baskets of ash wood. Pounding an ash log with a stone to loosen the fibrous layers was painstaking work. Later the layers had to be planed with a knife. "What good is that?" her mother used to complain, pointing to Sisul's wavy-edged strips. "If you don't make them straight and weave them together tight, they won't keep the animals away from your food."

During the next week the two of them had set to work making thread from the rind of wormseed plants that grew near a stream. Sisul silently protested that Mr. Finch had plenty of thread in his store. Why would she ever have to make her own thread? Yet, despite the growing impatience Sisul was beginning to show, Awatawessu pushed on to teach her daughter how to make animal traps.

Soon these afternoons began to feel endless to Sisul. She couldn't seem to keep her mind from wandering off to unexplored corners of the store, letting it travel over shelves of yard goods, spools of ribbons, then on to the doughnuts and cookies kept in huge, cavernous jars. There were pink cookies that looked like humped clouds of cotton with white, stringy snow scattered on top. If only her mother would let her try one of them, she thought, then she would know, and it would be over, finished. Instead, the cookies sat in her imagination, their flavor untested. Once she had timidly asked her mother if *she* had ever tasted one, and her mother had made an ugly sound with her mouth, as if she were spitting out poison. "White man's junk, no good," she said with contempt. That was no answer, Sisul muttered to herself. Had her mother ever actually tasted one?

Sisul liked to daydream about the radio, too. The

Osborns didn't have one, but Mr. Finch did, at the back of the store. It stood in the corner, a brown shiny box with knobs and cloth with gold thread. Music came out of it. There might be a singer, and you could catch the words and learn them. Weeks later fragments of the same songs would drift out an open window, and you could sing along, feeling important because you knew the words, too.

Then there were the people on the radio. She knew their names: Vic and Sade, Rush and Ma Perkins, David Harum. When Mr. Finch was busy she would peek around the back and study the glass tubes, which glowed red. Did those people live in there, she wondered? Were the little red tubes where Ma Perkins and her neighbors sat on rocking chairs and slammed doors inside tiny houses? She peered hard and almost convinced herself they were there, inside the glass, gesturing shadows. What would happen if she smashed the tubes? Would the people die, as if a terrible storm had struck? Perhaps they would survive and step over the glass, glad to be free, thanking her, shaking their heads in amazement. Or would they run off, frightened and squealing?

She wondered if there were any Indians inside the glass tubes. Surely Indians wouldn't be afraid of her. For that matter, Indians would be strong enough to get out by themselves if they wanted to. But she had never heard Indians talking on the radio, so she doubted that any of them lived in the tubes. The more she thought about it, the more she began to

18

doubt that anybody lived there. The glass tubes were probably just glass, that was all . . .

"Don't lose your knife," Awatawessu was saying. The solemn tone of her voice pulled Sisul away from her daydream. "Keep it sharp on gritty pebbles. You find them at the edge of a stream."

One day her mother had taken her into the high woods, her bright, deep-set eyes scanning the trees until she found a birch tree thick enough to suit her. "Winter bark is best," she said, smoothing her sinewy hand over the tree. "It comes off like skin. Today it won't be so easy, but I can't wait for winter."

(Had she meant "I'll be dead by winter," Sisul wondered later? Had her mother *known* then? Why hadn't she told her if she knew she was going to die? Was it forbidden to tell?)

Awatawessu took her knife out of her sweater pocket and made a deep cut around the tree. She grunted, then muttered, "Once I could do it the first time." She worked at it until beads of sweat came out on her forehead and her hand shook.

She handed Sisul the knife with a gesture of resignation. "Here, you must finish it," she said. She pointed to a place she had measured, two handwidths farther down the trunk from the first cut.

Sinking back against a rock, Awatawessu watched Sisul and encouraged her with little sounds. She was too tired, she said. Sisul would have to finish it alone. Sisul dug in with the knife, her tongue poking stiffly out of the corner of her mouth. Crying —

19

maybe because of a blister on her palm, but more likely, she thought later, because she was suddenly frightened to see her mother's weakness — she finished the job. Then, sick of it all, impatient to get it over with, she tried to pull the bark off. It cracked, and her mother had to push herself up and slowly, patiently, help her strip it away. Together they laid the bark out flat on the ground and Awatawessu marked a circle in the middle with the tip of her knife.

"Cut out the circle — then you'll be done," she said wearily. She sat down again, resting her head on her knee, coughing.

(What was she thinking then, Sisul asked herself. Was she afraid it might be the last time she'd be able to come to the woods with me? Was she listening to sounds — Sisul could hear them now: insects humming, rustling leaves, water flowing over stones — wondering how it would be, never to hear them again? Or *can* she hear them, Sisul wondered, even now?)

When she was finished, Awatawessu took up the bark and slipped it over Sisul's head, sandwiching her between the stiff stuff, letting her head poke through the cut-out circle like a turtle's.

"Now you have a new coat," her mother exclaimed, laughing a little. "The rain will run off, and you'll see, it will keep you warm. You could make thread and sew up the sides, but that makes it hard to wear. It's good this way." She stood back and admired the coat, her tired face suddenly flushed and full of life.

Sisul tried not to show dismay. The coat was scratchy and stiff. It was almost impossible to move in it. Did her mother really believe she would wear such a thing?

(The birch bark coat had been thrown out by Miss Osborn while Awatawessu lay sick. Sisul was relieved; she had been afraid she might be forced to wear it sometime. Miss Osborn didn't like Indian stuff littering the house, and it was finally burned for tinder one cold night.)

It was as if Awatawessu had been possessed, the way she'd insisted on teaching Sisul things, no matter how exhausted she felt, no matter how bored Sisul got. Once in a while — not often — she would finally respond to her daughter's restlessness, and taking a piece of birch, fold it over two or three times and bite hard into it, making tooth marks. Then she would open the bark up, pretend to look surprised, and exclaim over the designs her teeth had made, designs that could be rubbed and stained with grass or colored rock. Or she would devise a game by rolling balls of spruce gum down a board, clapping her hands enthusiastically whenever Sisul scored. "You can chew it, too," she said. "See, it's real gum. It even turns pink." (And you could pretend you had been treated to some of Mr. Finch's bubble gum, Sisul thought wistfully.)

But the games were boring, too. Her mother didn't

seem to understand that Sisul was not a child anymore, and not so easily amused.

Yet there was one thing her mother could do that always caught Sisul and made the moment come alive. "Sit next to me," Awatawessu would say. They would lean together against a tree and listen to the wind rush through the pine needles. She would put her arm around Sisul, whose shoulders were now broader than her own, and talk about Gluskabe, or about the Great Wind Bird, or about How Skunk Visited Gluskabe. Acting out the stories, changing her voice to a high wheedle to be Skunk, a low rasp to be Turtle, loosening her hair and flapping her arms to be the Wind Bird, she would sweep herself and her daughter along in a river of time and events that reached back to the very beginning of things. And Sisul would know then that nothing, nothing in the white man's world — no radios, no pink cookies, no shiny leather shoes — would ever count for anything against this vision into the flowing landscape of Wabanaki myth.

Alone, safe now from fears that had threatened to engulf her at the Osborns', Sisul leaned back on the flat rock. Supper was over. She couldn't think anymore. Remembered times with her mother, sights and sounds of death, scenes of shouting in the night, grew wavelike in her mind, then drew away. She slid down the rock and curled against it, pulling the blanket she'd stolen from the Osborns around her shoulders. Pine needles pricked her cheek and arms.

Tomorrow she would make a ground cover to keep out dampness and needles. Now she was too tired. She must remember to keep an eye out for a good stone to sharpen her knife on . . . she must start looking for thick birch trees to use for bark . . . above all, she must find a better place to stay. This one would do only for a night or two.

There was a lot to do if she was going to stay out here by herself. If . . . but it was no longer a question of *if*, was it? She would stay. Nothing could get her to go back to that house. She was going to cling to this mountainside even if she starved or froze.

What was hard to face, what she hardly dared think about — and yet couldn't help thinking about — was that there was no one anymore. That was the plain truth. No one in the world cared about her, whether she lived or died.

She couldn't say she felt frightened by this, or angry, or even very sad, for she felt her mother was still with her. Like a seed, the feeling of her lay dark inside. Her mother watched and cared, frowned now and then, a spirit lying within.

And yet — she ought to think about it! She was alone . . .

She shoved in closer to the rock. It was summer. Pine-scented air wound around her. The stars hung low. She could almost touch them. They were bright, like her mother's eyes.

Ranges of mountains erupting from the earth's crust all have their own identities —just as civilizations surrounding them build unique worlds while making a sometimes uneasy peace with their towering neighbors. Sometimes the mountain crests are beaten down, craggy; others loom as fierce, snarling animals. Others seem to gentle and soothe, like old grandmothers.

To those who know and love them, the mountains of New Hampshire appear as comfortable as old friends. Yet there are places and times when, like many an old friend, they may surprise you, as if to say, "Don't take me for granted —I may not always be as predictable as you expect." Those who know the mountains best understand this, and regard them with vigilance.

III

While eating breakfast the next morning Sisul laid out the contents of her basket and looked at them: Awatawessu's knife, its ornamented wood handle darkened by years of grime. Awatawessu's old tan sweater. She was going to have to get used to cold and must put off wearing the sweater as long as possible. A large box of Blue Diamond matches. This was probably her most valuable possession. Her mother had taught her how to start fires with sticks and dry moss, but it was tedious and never certain. Matches were essential. A hairbrush. She studied it for a moment. Bringing it along had been stupid; she ought to toss it away. It was part of the past that had to be choked off, now that she was living a strict Wabanaki existence. These four items, and the stolen blue blanket, were all she possessed.

Squatting and chewing on a lily root, she asked herself how she was to spend the day. Was it best to stay here, near the flat rock, and hunt for food? What if it rained? "Three foggy mornings bring rain," her mother used to say. There was no fog. Sisul looked up. The sky was almost cloudless. Even so, good shelter — that was the important thing. That and getting farther up the mountain. Best to be far away.

She dumped the knife, the matches, the sweater, and hairbrush into her basket, tied the blanket around her waist, and started off, feeling renewed. The stream, which had served her so well yesterday, would continue to be her guide.

Twice in the next hour she had to make detours around rock walls that blocked the way, fortresslike, forcing her to make twisted paths through woods thick with underbrush. Sisul was reminded of stories her mother used to tell about a stone face in the mountains. Probably the place her mother meant was far from here, yet as Sisul was suddenly confronted by a precipice that rose so high and appeared so wide, she could almost imagine that a craggy face was staring down at her. She was afraid she'd lose her way altogether if she tried to go around it.

Maybe she could wade through the stream — but no, it looked treacherous as it plunged through a cleft in the rock wall. Well, she'd have to climb the rock then. If it got bad, she could always come down and try something else.

The rock was a slope of the mountain itself, rough-hewn, furrowed with brows; as she slowly gained the top a view of tree spikes, then of far-off mountains, fell away from her.

With the wind blowing her hair back and chilling her face, she felt she had arrived at the top of the world. Yes, she was standing on it — she was a beacon, a spire, a piercing finger. Hidden down there lay the Osborn house and the village, and beyond that other villages, cities even. Then the sea . . . all at her feet. She flung out her arms and the wind buffeted her just as it buffeted the hard granite mountain. She felt that if she remained here she too could turn to stone and become timeless. There was glory in that: it would be good to stand unmoving while the wind blew, and rain and snow and ice and hot sun cracked and hit and tore at you.

Behind her the mountain leveled into a high valley before it rose again. Given a brief rest in its head-long race between flung-down boulders, the stream opened, handlike, into a small pond in the valley. A clearing lay beside it, a small green pasture on the mountainside.

Hard sensations of rock and weather and vast earth slid away from Sisul as she scrambled across the rock and made for this protected sunny place.

Here was her home! It had been created especially for her, this hidden green pasture and welcom-
ing pond. All the time it had been ready, waiting for
her to run away, cross the creek, follow the stream up
the mountainside. She threw herself down on the
warm, soft ground.

She was free, up in this high mountain valley! She
could breathe in the whole world! No more "Sisul
come here" or "Don't touch that." No more cower-
ing in her room, no more screams and slaps and
punches, no more strange sounds in the night.

She sat up and looked around. There was a treasure house of good food here — lilies, sumac, berry
bushes, even cattails at the edge of the pond. She
saw herself coming into the morning sunshine from
the opening of a cave in a nearby wood. Day would
follow day; her hours would be filled with gathering
food and hot noontime rests. She could swim in the
pond when she felt like it and make piles of smooth
pebbles from the stream bottom . . . cool evenings
wafted past, quiet suppers at the entrance of the
cave, sounds of the high woods were lulling her to
sleep . . . It would grow cold, but there were fires to
keep her warm. Wood was already neatly stacked
beside a stone fireplace that had built itself inside
her head.

She spent two long days searching for the cave she
had imagined that morning. Late on the afternoon of
the second day she almost stumbled into a large, hollowed-out spot in the ground that was sheltered by

an overhanging rock ledge. The place was hidden by low, brushy branches of a hemlock group. It was not a real cave, true, but back underneath, where rock and earth met, it was as dry and concealed as one. The sides were open, of course — Sisul told herself it was like having the windows open on a summer day — but in time she could hang bark or boughs there to help protect herself from bad weather. Altogether it would be a good shelter, almost a cave. She decided to call it one, anyway.

Weeks flew by. The weather was mostly good, as one silken August day glided into another. There were always new chores to attend to now that she had a home of her own, and every night before falling asleep she would draw up a list in her mind of what had to be done the next day. Food, as she had guessed, was plentiful; she had only to teach herself not to crave bread and meat. It was too soon to make a fire, she decided, so there was no point in trying to catch any game.

Fish could be eaten raw, however, so one afternoon she patiently bent over the stream and, using her hands, tried to catch a trout that hovered in a cold deep spot. But the old fellow was much too clever — she would have to do it properly and rig up a pole with a hook and bait. Meanwhile she contented herself with crayfish. Once, but only once, she dreamed of huge platefuls of bread and butter, sopping with beef gravy.

Gradually she began to break into the wilderness around her, slowly making it hers. Down the mountain a bit, in front of the rock face, grew a glowing stand of birches, several of them thick enough to provide good sheets of bark. When October came she would be showered with acorns from a big white oak that stood in the field on the other side of the stream. Upstream the sun-scattered water flushed over rocks, and tiny minnows disappeared like running gold when her shadow touched them. A mossy place deep in the forest was greenly cool on hot days; in the dusk weasels slunk by there, and sometimes deer. Forest sounds grew comfortable to her, and she no longer woke up at night when a neighboring screech owl called.

The nights had grown longer, she noticed, and days were sometimes not so warm. The impending cold began to worry her. Her heart pounded a little when she tried to imagine what winter would be like. Was this really happening, she sometimes stopped and asked herself. Was she really going to stay here by herself through a freezing, icy winter? Could she do it?

Almost as if in answer to that question, she began to feel she was not alone. The feeling grew in her daily; sometimes she found herself stealing through the woods, peering over her shoulder into shadowy interiors. One morning when she woke up the sensation was keener than ever. She brushed it aside impatiently. She had more important things to concern her on this day: she was bringing a stove down to her cave.

So far her biggest problem had been keeping animals away from her food. A carefully laid-in supply was slowly dwindling, thanks to a growing, courageous brigade of mice, squirrels, chipmunks, otters, mink. Their ranks grew each day. A porcupine rattled around on the stone ledge every night, sniffing hungrily. She knew she ought to make more and more food baskets, but just thinking about the hard work of planing ash logs and cutting straight-edged strips was tiring, and she kept putting it off.

Salvation came when she stumbled across an old metal stove lying on its side among some charred timbers on the other side of the stream. Someone must have had a cabin there years back. At first it was hard for her to accept the idea that she had not been the first to discover this mountain valley, and the sight of the ruins actually made her angry. But as she stood poking at the stove with her foot, pushing the oven door open and closed, it occurred to her that the stove would make a perfect cabinet for her food. The next few days had been devoted to getting the stove over to her cave. Today she was determined to get it all the way home.

Suddenly, as she knelt down to start shoving, a feeling blazed over her that someone was near. She *had* heard something this time, she was sure! She stood up, straining her ears; again silence. Yet why had the vision of a lumber camp passed through her mind? Had she heard the faint sound of an ax? If so, she didn't hear it again. Only the silence of midday hung over her. She gave up listening and went back to work.

Late that afternoon the stove, having received its last push, slid into the cave, rocks and dirt tumbling down with it. For a long time Sisul was too exhausted to do more than sit and stare at the rusty black hulk.

How good to be able to rest in her own place! Sore and tired, she lay back on her birch bark ground cover and sighed deeply. It surprised her to discover slow tears creeping from the corners of her eyes. She felt them crawl down her cheeks, then drop into her hair. Was she so unhappy? she asked herself.

Why else did people cry, if not from unhappiness, or pain, or anger? Never before had she experienced such a gentle sadness ... an awareness of time passing, loneliness, of early happiness forever gone. It was not altogether unpleasant, crying like this. Something important seemed to be happening, something deep and stirring, as if she were telling herself that her life was changing, that she would never again be the young girl she had been. She lay there, her cheeks cooling under evaporating tears, until the skittering sounds of chipmunks reminded her that there was work to do.

After she had arranged all the food on the oven shelves, separating the nuts and roots and berries, each group in its own section, and had heard the oven door close with a satisfying bang, she got under her blanket and lay back again, watching the late afternoon light glint through shifting needles across the front of the cave. Wind stirred the tops of the pines; inside everything was still.

Once again the melancholy feeling drifted over her. It had never left, really; now it no longer seemed so sweet. What was wrong with her! This was the time she ought to be feeling jubilant, not discontented and restless.

But there was so much stillness. Was she hungering for human murmuring, friendly laughter? Ha, she ought to be grateful for the stillness! How different a stillness it was from the attic room at the Osborns', where the dead silences suffocated you. She remembered how she used to imagine that old echoes were hovering over the silence, up by the ceiling, moving restlessly around the eaves, waiting to scream out.

Here there was peace. The shifting play of seasons changing, of sunlight hidden, then bursting from behind heavy pine boughs, of animals darting across the forest floor and open fields, of birds in flight and nesting — there were a thousand frail threads that made the web of each day different from every other — surely all this ought to satisfy her, or anyone, for a lifetime. How dare she be sad or lonely! What was wrong with her . . .

She jumped up suddenly, hitting her head on the rock ledge. That was a noise, an ax hitting wood! This time there was no doubt.

She crawled outside and heard the ax again, then again and again, its sound ringing across the evening air. So there it was — it was a fact that she was not alone. Should she go now and find out where the sound came from? No — it was growing dark, she could get lost; she'd better wait until morning.

All through supper she could feel her heart pounding, first in eager anticipation, then, as she thought about what might come of all this, in fear. If there was a lumber camp farther up the mountain she might have to get away fast.

All night she tossed and turned, her ears straining for more sound, her thoughts in turmoil, until in the early morning she finally dropped off to sleep.

When she awoke the sun was already ablaze. She stuffed down some breakfast and ran off in the direction she thought the noise had come from — farther up the mountain, toward the east. All along the way she kept imagining she saw a lumberman's plaid shirt between the trees.

Around noontime she finally discovered the source of the noise. Because she was looking for something quite different from what in fact was there, she almost walked into the view of a man standing on a bluff overlooking the stream. A brown, shaggy-coated goat was feeding next to him and a couple of chickens scratched around in the dirt. Behind him was perched a tarpaper shack, a pipe chimney sticking out of the roof.

She ducked behind a rock and watched, as the man, wearing faded blue work clothes and carrying a saw and ax, made his way down a steep path to the stream. He came down the path wearily, and as he drew closer she could see that his face was worn by many years of sun and wind. His thin white hair seemed to catch and play with the bright noon sun.

What was he doing way up here?

Now he was pushing farther upstream, away from her, and soon she heard his ax. She stood up, took one last look at him — a patch of blue moving up and down in rhythm to the sound of the ax — and, pondering the meaning of this new discovery, went back to the cave.

She decided that the only thing she could do was to keep out of sight and never let him know she was here. It was lucky he hadn't spotted her before she had discovered him! Was there any reason why he would wander down to her part of the mountain? If she started a fire he'd be sure to notice the smoke and probably come to investigate. She tried to think of ways to camouflage a fire: she knew which kinds of wood made less smoke than others, and thought that on windy days most of the smoke would be scattered before it got above the tree tops, where it could be seen. She would have to experiment — but on another part of the mountain, far from her place and his.

She wondered what had made him choose this mountain to live on. Would he go away when winter came? Surely the shack was only a summer place. If so, maybe she could move in during the hard part of the winter. Why not? She saw herself breaking into the cabin as snow whirled around the windows, hauling in wood, and warming herself in front of a crackling fire.

Perhaps the morning's discovery wasn't so terrible

after all. She felt that someone, some thing, was beckoning to her — had called her up to this mountain, brought her to the pasture, and was allowing her now to discover, like the center of an unfolding flower, this place of future safety and warmth.

IV

The man was working on his dam the first time he noticed her. She was standing behind the beech tree that grew on the other side of the stream, her faded cotton dress paler even than the smooth bark. He thought he'd better not pay any attention to her, and pretended to gaze off at the mountain top.

Turning back to work, he asked himself if he'd have started the dam if he'd known — really *known* — what backbreaking work it was going to be. Here he was, sweaty and aching, pushing rock loads down to the dam site. For two solid weeks now, once the regular daily chores were finished, he'd been chopping and splitting logs, hauling and dumping rock, cursing out loud in exasperation and fatigue. He forced himself to jostle one more load of rocks into place across the stream bed. In a minute he'd have to start swinging his ax again to make more logs for the dam's surface.

He sat back on his heels, noisily blowing out his breath. That girl was still behind the beech tree, watching him. Thin, with dirty knees, black hair, and two coal eyes. Maybe part Indian, about twelve or so. Again he turned away.

October was here and he'd meant to have the dam finished by now, but it had taken most of the wretched summer just to clear land for the pond. Eighty-six trees, scrub pine and maple, had come down. Each one of them, he thought ruefully, was a monument to his aching muscles. Now eighty-six stumps erupted from the underbrush like raw sores. At times he longed for snow to cover the whole ugly mess so he could forget about it until next spring. But no, dammit, even if it killed him, that dam was going to get finished before winter set in. It was a goal he'd set himself. He spat. His muscles felt even worse now that they weren't warm and working. He groaned and forced himself back to work, wondering if this was what rheumatism was.

His name was Bruce, and he had lived alone on the mountain for sixteen years. Exactly when he'd decided to stay there for the rest of his life he could no longer remember. At first the mountain had been just a temporary refuge, a place to lick his wounds and get some peace and a view of himself after getting out of prison.

He'd always been attracted to these New Hampshire mountains. As a boy he'd hungered for them all winter long while he stared out his bedroom window at the dirty snow piled in the streets. Years later in his prison cell he would wake up, dry-mouthed, after dreaming of cool black forests.

After prison he'd intended to camp out on Prentiss Mountain only for a few months, then leave for Chicago or San Francisco and start a new life. But the day of departure kept getting put off.

Even when cold weather drove him off the mountain he still couldn't seem to leave New Hampshire, and began taking odd jobs in the village. This was hard to do because everybody down there knew he'd just spent fourteen years in prison. It was only natural for people to be suspicious, and only natural for him to resent it. He forced himself to stick it out, though, because a plan was slowly taking shape in his mind. Every time he was tempted to hop on a train for the West, his imagination pulled him back to a certain place on the mountain where just below the highest peak a flat bluff overlooked a rushing stream.

Most of the mountain belonged to the Prentiss brothers, who worked in a mill in Manchester. Bruce wrote to them, and after a month of checking an empty mailbox every day, he finally found a letter saying they'd be willing to sell him forty acres for $200.

He told himself it wasn't smart to rush into anything. Yet he thought there wasn't much risk involved — he could probably just survive on the interest from his mother's insurance money. Why not give it a try for a year?

So he bought the land. By early spring, with snow still on the ground, he'd already made several trips up to the bluff, pulling a toboggan loaded with tools, building supplies, some books, and what he hoped was a year's stock of staple food. All that year he made mistakes about gardening, preserving food, putting a tarpaper roof over a pine-board frame. He kept saying to himself, "Next time I'll do it this way; next time I'll know better." Without even trying, he made the decision to stay on for at least one more year. He brought up a goat and a few chickens. By the end of the second year he no longer thought about leaving.

Bruce had never thought he would be a happy man. Very early he'd started looking at life as something to be endured, something to get through as best you could. But here on Prentiss Mountain he found himself waking up each day eager to feel again those moments when his body and the work it did would slip into a rhythm that nature so generously provided. He began to feel he was as rightful a part of the mountain as the rocks and soil and trees. Life was no longer a struggle against something. Up here he was struggling *for* something, with nature as his ally. The mountain had given him a soul; he would never, never leave it.

Would he be lonely, he wondered at first? In prison he used to cry out for someone to hold and talk to. By the time half his term was over he'd gotten used to pushing the cries down, thinking that when he got free he'd probably find someone. But he must have held himself back too long, because after prison he still wouldn't let himself yearn for human companionship. If he ever felt like pouring out his feelings, he immediately by-passed the urge by throwing himself into some new project.

Maybe that was why he'd started on the dam. Early one morning last spring he'd been lying in bed, half awake, when he heard the distant honking of Canada geese. He ran out and saw them up high, eight of them silhouetted against the gray dawn sky on their yearly journey to breeding ponds far north. Sometimes he thought about traveling to wild-sounding places like Labrador and Hudson Bay — it struck him that those lone stretches of scrub tree waste, ice, and melting snow would be a fitting place for him; there would be winter nights that never ended, gray and cold, and in the summer a kind of magic sunlight that never ceased. What strange forms of life grew there? And what kind of strange man was he to want to go there, he thought as he stood shivering in the cold morning air.

It occurred to him that if he made a dam and a pond right here in the little valley formed by the stream, he might be able to attract some geese to his own place. They might stay for at least a week or two each spring and fall. Somehow it would make him feel in touch with the wild loneliness of the distant north. Anyway, it was something to do.

Now, seven months later, he was so bone tired that getting up each morning was an act of will. Only the memory of the geese in flight, pushing ahead like eight lonely hunters, kept him going.

The sun fell behind the trees as he hauled the last load of rocks, and a chill hit his back as he shoved the wheelbarrow into place at the dam site. "I'm getting too old for this," he said to himself. Once the sun went down at this time of year there was never any doubt that winter was waiting, an icy threat holding on at the edge. He straightened up painfully and stretched. He was sure he hadn't thought of her all afternoon, but he found himself looking toward the beech tree to see if the girl was still there.

What in God's name brought her up this high on the mountain, he wondered. Had she come just to get a look at him? He supposed he was still talked about now and then down in the village. It would be interesting to know what stories kids were told about him. Maybe this girl had come up on a dare, and now she'd go running home, full of breathless revelations about the crazy old jailbird up on the mountain. Anyway, it looked as if she'd left, which was just as well, considering the long hike she had to get home.

V

Fall was underway. Awatawessu had called it Leaf-Reddening Month. It was a pretty name, Sisul thought; better than October.

A mood of happy survival reigned in Sisul's domain, a busy rush to get set for winter: laying in piles of extra food, drying the last batch of berries and apples in the sun, building up stacks of firewood in different parts of the forest. Later, when she had more time, she would tie spruce root around bundles of wood and hang them from branches so they'd be above the deep snow.

Sisul was sure her mother must be proud of her. Often in the past few weeks Awatawessu had actually appeared to her. She came either as a softly blurred smiling face, surrounded by dark sunlit hair, or as a hushed voice singing a soothing, rocking song. The singing always began with a long sigh, usually when Sisul was busy digging roots under the sun or stripping a berry bush. Sisul would freeze and lift her head, listening to what sounded like Indian words struggling through water or thick air. If she tried to listen too hard, though, the sounds faded away.

Awatawessu's face also presented itself at odd, busy moments, and when Sisul tried to penetrate the blurry softness and block out the sunlight shimmering around black hair, the face melted away, a wisp of fog swallowed by sunlight.

Sisul never questioned these appearances. She had always assumed that her mother, or more likely her mother's spirit, existed up in the sky, and what was more natural than for Awatawessu to be in touch with her daughter? Unfortunately, it seemed impossible for them actually to talk to each other, although there were plenty of times when Sisul carried on imaginary conversations, talking out loud to her mother and pretending she could hear Awatawessu's replies.

The give-and-take of conversation was something Sisul began to miss. Sometimes she tried to make a chipmunk listen, could almost believe it *was* listening, until it scurried away abruptly in the middle of a

44

sentence or, worse, at the climax of a story.

At first Sisul was afraid that the white-haired man would find her, but as the weeks passed, with no sign of him in her territory, she stopped worrying. On the trail of some sumac one day she found herself near him. Stream water swirled around his boots, his sinewy arms glistened, he grunted and swore to himself, seeing nothing but his work. It was both fascinating and frightening to watch him. Except for occasional visits to Mr. Finch's store, Sisul had rarely had a chance to see other people because she'd always had to stay up at the Osborns' to help her mother. Never had she seen such a strong old man before. "An old *awenotc*," her mother would have called him. That was what Awatawessu always called people who weren't Indians.

Yet he was another person — real, not imaginary. In spite of her fear, Sisul was drawn to him and began to hope she would come across him again. Finally she began going up to his place on purpose. Sometimes she spent as much as an hour watching him, despite warnings from her Indian conscience.

This afternoon she was hiding behind the beech tree directly across the stream from where he worked. She'd never dared to come so close before, and stood unmoving, questioning herself. What was so interesting about him? Why waste a whole afternoon watching him? She must run down to the field and do the job she'd been looking forward to for many weeks. Do it now, she told herself sternly.

It was a vision of autumn-bright leaves on a white

oak tree that was trying to call her away. Some of the leaves were turning brown; many of them had already fallen. Hidden among them would be a crop of good sweet acorns. She sighed, slowly pulled herself away, and went back downstream. Soon she was at work, seeking out capped brown nuts among the maple leaves. By the time she had as many as she could carry, the sun was down. In her white cotton dress she looked like a small ghost slipping through the hanging boughs of hemlock toward home. The darkening forest closed around her. She felt weightless, like a handful of dark air.

Inside the shadowy interior of her cave she shoved the acorns into the corner of the oven, then groped for a few cattail shoots and began to gnaw on them. She leaned back, chewing slowly. Supper could wait tonight. Crouching forward again, she opened the bottom drawer of the stove and reached way into the rear. Her fingers grasped the brush and drew it out.

It was the same hairbrush she had brought along in her basket. Splendidly displayed on the dresser in Miss Osborn's room, along with a matching mirror and comb, to the best of Sisul's knowledge it had never been used. The honey-colored wooden handle was carved in a hand-fitting way, and glistening on its back was a scene of a little house with black-shuttered windows, a blue door, and a red chimney from which smoke curled perfectly into the blue sky. Around the cottage grew a sunny garden of hollyhocks and larkspur. Standing there, her wide hoop skirt partly hidden by the flowers, was a girl whose

46

golden hair hung in corkscrew curls under a straw bonnet. Some paint had chipped away through the years: part of the girl's face was gone as well as the left wall of the house.

Sisul crawled to the opening of the cave to study the picture in the faint twilight. Who was this pretty girl, she always asked herself. Had she ever been alive? Had the flowers really grown in some past time? She, Sisul, could make them come to life! She closed her eyes and heard the insects buzz around the blossoms. Some of the blooms were wilting in the hot sun; they surrounded her — *she* was the girl, and inside the shuttered house a mother and father waited for her. Now they called out, telling her it was too hot in the garden; she must come inside. Her hand reached out and lightly touched the flowers before she turned toward the blue door, which pushed itself open and revealed to her a dark, cool room with curtains fluttering at the windows. She moved soundlessly through wallpapered rooms, slowly, slowly, up the stairs, down the hallway, to the room that always lay at the end. The room contained a closet. Closed inside it were dresses, pink and yellow and blue ones, ready to burst out of their prison. She had only to open the door and the skirts would spring out, all ruffles and lace and ribbons ... but why was there smoke coming out of the chimney?

That ruined it, every time. A hot day, flowers blooming, butterflies hovering — and smoke curling out of a chimney! The picture was a fake. Unless they were burning trash. But people didn't burn trash in fireplaces, especially in summertime. It was done outside. There was no explanation for the smoke. The house with the shutters, the girl in the garden — none of it was real.

She shoved the brush away. Resolute, she made herself imagine the Indian world her mother had tried to create for her. Somewhere in the north there was a *real* place called Wachussami, not a painted, made-up scene. Before her mother had gotten so sick she used to dream with Sisul about going back. "Everyone will be so surprised . . . They will laugh and your old grandmother will give us a feast . . ."

It used to upset Awatawessu when Sisul said she couldn't remember anything about Wachussami. "Don't you even remember your grandmother's house? The river, the orange rocks down by the sea?"

Now in the cave Sisul closed her eyes and tried to look back into that distant time when she was little more than a baby. Here and there she could catch a flicker of light illuminating a corner with shadows and half-seen people. Someone was cracking a walnut; she could almost see the old brown hand that held a broken nut meat out to her while firelight glowed in a dark winter afternoon. Did the old hand belong to her grandmother? Suddenly someone grabbed her and lifted her up high and swung her around; a man laughed, and firelight danced off his shining face. A silver belt buckle caught the light, and the light traveled to his teeth and eyes. Who was that man? Was he her father?

Sisul opened her eyes. The night had turned chilly. She pulled on the tan sweater and wrapped the blanket around her shoulders. It was time to provide herself with warmer clothing now that cold weather was coming. Instead of sitting here daydreaming she ought to be making plans for catching some rabbits.

Catching any animal was not going to be easy, and that was only the first step. The dead carcass would have to be skinned, the skin dried and stretched and scraped, the pieces sewn together. She wasn't sure she could do it, especially since the job would have to be repeated again and again if she was to have enough fur for a coat or even a jacket.

Sisul went to the entrance of the cave. The woods were dark now. Bright stars shifted through the tops of the pine trees. "Go on, call him," she heard her mother say. "Gluskabe, the hunter among the stars, call him — he will help you."

What did her mother mean, call Gluskabe! How could someone who had turned into stars help her, shivering down here in a hole under a rock? She crawled back inside and rolled herself up in the blanket. She would skip supper tonight; she was too tired, too impatient . . .

Awatawessu's voice followed her. "Your ancestors were great hunters," her mother insisted, "the best hunters there ever were. A rabbit, a big rabbit, with soft fur, so thick and warm. There he is! Catch him, catch him!"

Sisul felt herself being lifted out of the cave.

Stretching out her arms, she caught hold of a huge rabbit, his thick fur enveloping her. She held tight and the rabbit carried her through the moonlit forest, silently up the valley floor and up to the mountain top, where a rock glistened like black ice in the moonlight. Then the rabbit leaped into the sky itself, and she crouched on his back, holding tight, sinking into the thick fur, feeling his warm blood pound beneath her arms, and he grew bigger and bigger and they soared higher and higher until they were in the stars and the giant rabbit was carrying her among them, noiselessly, and on and on they rode until even the moon was a small shining stone beneath them, out toward Gluskabe . . .

VI

Bruce had fed and milked Selgie, his goat, and was
coming out of his tarpaper shack to get the day's load
of firewood when he looked up and saw snow blowing across the black rocks at the top of the mountain.
The snow worried him, coming so early. November
wasn't even here yet. He thought about putting off
making bread until tomorrow and going down to the
stream right now to finish the core of the dam. "Let
the bread-making go," he said to himself. "If tomor-

row brings bad weather you'll be glad to have work to keep you busy inside."

But no, that wouldn't do. Long ago, when he'd decided to stay on the mountain, he realized the only way to survive was to set a routine and make himself follow it, no matter what; nature would get the best of him and beat him down if he didn't. He had had to become a strong master to himself.

He sighed and got out the basin for mixing dough, took out the starter from an earthenware crock, dumped in flour and water, and began mixing the dough with weatherbeaten hands.

An hour later all the regular chores that had to get done that day were finished, so by midmorning he was free to pull on his heavy boots and scramble down the embankment to the dam, where he set to work until lunch time.

A little way uphill a high boulder of rough granite jutted into the stream; he liked to sit up there in fair weather to eat lunch. When the sun was at high noon a hushed silence often fell over the woods, as if life were resting, panting softly in secluded nests and holes. The glory of fall, he noticed — the lit-up oranges and reds and yellows — was pretty well over by now. Sometimes a damp chill, a whiff of snow, would sneak in through the crispness. He always felt an extreme sadness at this time of year, but his sadness mingled with something sharp and invigorating. It was an odd combination, he thought — profound melancholy and aroused vigor, all tied up in some mysterious fashion with the way a person's body answered to the weather.

He sat in the sun a while longer, allowing himself a last pipeful of tobacco before getting back to work. As he puffed thoughtfully, the image of the girl standing behind the beech tree suddenly came into his head, and gradually he became convinced that she was there again today, watching him. He squinted into the hemlock trees across the stream.

"What are you doing out there?" he called out suddenly. His voice sounded gruff to him. He wasn't used to talking so that anybody could hear him.

He listened, but there was no sign of her. Still, he was sure she was there. Had a sound revealed her to him, a flash of something not quite seen?

"Are you hungry?" he shouted, and slid off the rock and climbed up the hill to his shack. A few minutes later he came back out, carrying some bread and cheese in his hands and a piece of chicken wire tucked under his arm. He crossed the stream and strode over to the beech tree, wrapped the bread and cheese carefully in the wire, and hung the package on a dead branch.

"If you're hungry, here's something for you," he called out.

Later, back at work again, he caught a flicker of white among the trees. As soon as he bent his head and pretended to push a rock into place, he saw her come out and grab the wire basket and slip silently back into the woods.

"Now I've done it," he thought, dismayed. Why was he encouraging her to hang around? What was she doing up here, anyway? It was the third time he'd seen her in as many weeks. He ought to have a talk with her, tell her to stay away. If she came back again, that's what he was going to do.

Sisul kept telling herself it was dangerous to take the food. For what seemed an eternity she had stared at the bread and cheese hanging in its little wire basket. She almost made herself walk away and leave it. Then suddenly she couldn't stand it any longer and dashed in and grabbed the food off the branch. Moments later she was settling down with her feast in a mossy clearing and cramming down the coarse homemade bread and strong goat cheese. Half was gone before she made herself eat one piece at a time so as to relish each morsel, saving and licking every tiny crumb off her fingers. When it was finally gone she stretched back on the soft moss and, bite by bite, lived over the last five minutes. Who could have imagined such pleasure in a piece of bread!

She turned over and studied some moss. So she'd been wrong in thinking the man hadn't seen her. How long had he known about her? What would he do now that he *did* know? Would he start asking people about her? What if he found out she belonged to the Osborns? Had he put the food out just to tempt her into coming close so he could get a good look at her?

What a stupid thing she'd done! She would never go back there again, not until winter had set in and the man was gone for good. Angry with herself, she walked back downstream to her cave, kicking at pebbles, breaking off dead branches along the way.

This afternoon she was going to catch some rabbits. The noose, made out of tightly woven bass wood strips, was finished. She knew where the rabbits had a runway; now all that remained was to set up a cross stick on two forked branches and hang the noose from it.

Soon she was sitting propped up against a stone about thirty feet from the rabbits' runway, waiting for her first catch. As the minutes passed she began thinking about Gluskabe. Did he know everything, that old hunter who was not quite human? He wasn't exactly God, either. Only God (so Miss Osborn said) knew everything. Yet Gluskabe (Awatawessu used to say) had made the Wabanakis and all the animals. Had God made Gluskabe? Or was it the other way around?

"Gluskabe came first into this country," her mother used to say, "into Nova Scotia, Maine, Canada, all the wild country to the north, where we come from, the land next to the sunrise . . . The land of the sunrise, the land of the Wabanaki . . ." Her mother seemed to like to say the words, almost as if they were magic, over and over to herself . . . the land of the sunrise, the land of the Wabanaki . . .

"One morning," she went on, "Gluskabe took his bow and arrows and shot at trees, the same ash trees that are good for making baskets. Indians came out of the bark; he made an Indian from every tree.

"Then he made all the animals. At first they were very large." Awatawessu laughed. "That was a big mistake because when Gluskabe said to the moose, 'What would you do if you saw an Indian coming?' the moose said, 'I'd pull the trees down on him,' and so Gluskabe very quick made the moose smaller. Even so, old moose is still pretty big. I think he left him that way because there's so much good meat on him.

"Even the squirrel was big in those days, bigger than a bear. But Gluskabe took him in his hands and smoothed him down until he got smaller and smaller. Then the squirrel turned into Gluskabe's dog, and when he wanted it to, it would grow big again and kill his enemies for him.

"The white bear Gluskabe sent off north to the land of rocks and ice, but when he asked the brown bear what he would do if he met a man, the bear said, 'I would be afraid and run,' so Gluskabe left the brown bear alone. The rabbit he spread all over the earth for man to hunt and eat, and that's why there are so many, even today . . ."

"Maybe there are," Sisul thought, "but none seem to be coming this way." Sighing, she leaned back and looked at the sky. It was tiring, sitting here without moving and with nothing to look at or listen to. The sky today was almost as blue as the sky on the back of the brush. Ah, the brush . . . she would imagine herself to be the pretty girl now, out for a walk in the woods behind the shuttered cottage ... Wide ruffled skirts spread around her and she took off her straw bonnet and fanned herself. It was so hot here; if only the bugs would leave her alone! ... Ah yes, she had almost forgotten the lovely cookies Mamma had made for her. Chocolate and butter, weren't they? With pink frosting. What else was in the little box? A juicy apple, some berries, and a thick ham sandwich. Way, way down in the very bottom of the basket was a whole handful of colored candies. Here was a yellow one, a red one, a green one, an orange one ... One by one she imagined dropping them into her hand, trying to decide which to pop into her mouth first ...

Once Mr. Finch had given Sisul a candy like that, a yellow one, and she had been surprised at how sweet and sour it was at the same time. Tears had come to her eyes as she'd chewed it. Later she found out you were supposed to suck it and let it give off its juice for as long as you could make it last. She had been furious. Why hadn't anyone told her, so she could have gotten the best out of that one chance? But who was there to tell her? There was only Awatawessu, and what had she known about such things?

Now, in her imagination, Sisul was going to eat it the right way. She knew just how it would feel, all the juicy sourness pouring into her mouth. Which color? Red? No, better not. She wasn't sure how a red one tasted. It would have to be yellow again.

She picked it up between her fingers and placed it on the top of her tongue. There it was, all sour and juice . . .

A rabbit! He was caught, his little back legs pushing furiously as he tried to free himself. Sisul hurried over and grabbed him. He crouched in her tight grasp, stiff with fear, his ears flat against his head. The sight and feel of him begged her to let him go, but she didn't allow herself to think of that, and taking Awatawessu's knife, she plunged the blade in at the place where she thought his heart was. She felt his lean body struggle for a moment, then go limp.

She knelt and stared at him for a long time, although she was not really seeing him or thinking about him. Her mind was a blank and she was aware only of the softness of his body against her hands. Eventually she began to notice the blood on her hands. It felt sticky. She picked up the carcass by the ears, carried it hurriedly to her cave, covered it with hemlock boughs, then ran to the stream and lay over a rock on her stomach, washing her hands in the dark water.

When she relaxed her hands, the water pushed them forward and cups of air, like five silver fishes, danced off the ends of her fingers. How peaceful it was to stretch out here and listen to water flowing over stones — repeated sounds, over and over, yet never exactly the same — all the different water sounds slipping over and around the rocks and disappearing down the mountain. You could fall asleep on this rock; the water sounds would fade drowsily away . . .

She thought, "I have to get the skin off him."

Blood was caked in the white fur of his breast. Her hands, still cold from the water, burrowed into the fur and felt along the ears, now rigid. For a moment she thought, "He's dead, he will never run again," but she shook her head as if to shake the thought away, and made herself begin to cut off the skin. The knife should have been sharper — it was making jagged, rough slashes. More and more impatient to get the job over with, she began cutting too fast, any old way. How was she to go through this again and again in order to make even a jacket, much less a coat? It was impossible, she could never do it. Suddenly she couldn't stand it, and tossing the knife aside, she took the carcass and threw it from her, over into some bushes. No fur coat. That ended it.

Inside the cave that night she turned over and lay on her back, staring out at the patches of night sky through the trees. She thought about the hunters of long ago, her own great-grandfathers and great-uncles running silently through the woods, arrows singing across the still afternoon air, striking into the hearts of deer and moose. Did anyone cry out? What did these hunters feel, watching their prey die on those distant afternoons?

A vision of Gluskabe rose before her, his tall body gliding toward her through the woods. She could see him stopping outside her cave, poised, his bow and arrow ready for the faint stir that would betray an animal's hiding place. Suddenly *she* was the wild animal, and Gluskabe, her own ancestor, was the hunter. She dared not breathe in case he heard and knelt down to find her hidden under the rock ledge, and her stomach ached with the strain of holding her breath.

After that first time Gluskabe came almost every night, and to crawl back into the cave and try to get to sleep was almost more than she could endure, although in daylight hours she knew she was imagining everything. Why should she be afraid of Gluskabe? Wasn't he hers, in a way? She was Indian and so was he. Yet fear mounted inside her and by nightfall always persuaded her that Gluskabe was really coming to get her. On dry nights she began to sleep outside the cave. But soon the nights grew so cold she found herself caught between the terror of becoming Gluskabe's prey and the misery of cold.

Then one night, lying curled up in the back of the cave, sensing that Gluskabe had crept up to the opening, she called out angrily, "Go away!" She held her breath. Nothing happened, and suddenly she knew he was gone. "Go away!" she yelled again, then began to laugh because it sounded funny to hear her own voice in the black silence. "Go away, go away," she whispered over and over to herself until the words turned into a chant, a lullaby to herself.

After that night she discovered she could always keep Gluskabe away by singing before she fell asleep.

VII

A stranger walking by Sisul's cave on those early November nights would have been startled to hear singing in the middle of the wilderness, and if the stranger believed in the supernatural, he might have convinced himself that he was hearing — what? A wood nymph? A forest witch weaving her song of enchantment over rocks and streams and tree trunks?

Except for Bruce, however, nobody ever came to Sisul's wooded mountainside, and when he happened to hear Sisul singing herself to sleep one night, he had few doubts about what he was hearing.

He had gone out on the porch to sit for a moment in the strangely mild night before turning in. It was almost as if the soft air of summer had come back for one curious look around before moving on. A full moon was rising behind the cabin, and Bruce felt his mind rise and begin to float along with it, letting him look far beyond the present moment. He saw his lifetime as a mere flicker; something like the quick leap of an insect on a vast field. Was that all life was, he thought? A trivial — if valiant — hop before disappearing into the ground?

A twinge of remorse flared up. What about it, living up here, cut off from people, so aloof, like a solitary rock? Was this what he was on earth for?

It was an old argument, one he'd been carrying on with himself for many years. During prison he had started reading for the first time in his life; some of the books posed questions he'd never thought about before — or if he had thought of them, he'd quickly turned them off with a shrug or a "who cares?"

Now he couldn't seem to stop questioning himself. "What am I doing with my life?" he would ask. "Are we born just so we can spend a certain number of years scrambling for food and shelter; then we die?

"At least I'm not doing anyone any harm — that's something," he would say to himself wearily. "Down below, who knows what I might have become? I could have killed a man once, idiot that I was."

For the thousandth time he wondered if he really believed that. He'd been pretty young. But that was no excuse. As he looked back and tried to remember what was going through his head then, he thought he must have been like some dumb animal gone crazy, unable to control itself as it headed irrevocably toward disaster. Surely he would never have shot that poor frightened store clerk.

He sighed deeply and tried to shake the stale memories out of his head. It was better to think about what he'd accomplished on the mountain. Well, what about that? What was so wonderful, after all, about what he'd done here? When he'd first come there had been a clear cold stream running down from the mountain top, threading a course between the white birches and dark evergreens. That was all. Now there were many fewer trees, his shack, some unavoidable human and animal litter, and the dam. He had spoiled something — had rubbed a dirty, clumsy thumb across a jewellike painting. But, he argued to himself, everything would grow back when he died — the trees would seed themselves and cover the bare spots, the tarpaper shack would crumble and turn to rot in the forest loam, the dam would give way some year after a high spring flood, and ten or fifteen years after he was dead there would be few signs of his having been here. That was the way he wanted it.

The night was quiet. Summer's insects had vanished into their cocoons, their tree cracks, their warm pockets in the subsoil. He turned his senses outward and saw a forest being shaped out of the darkness across the stream, each spike-topped tree coming coolly aglow as moonlight struck. He got up from his chair, stretched, and decided to take a walk before turning in.

Over the current of wind rushing back and forth uneasily through the pine trees he could hear dry noises of the night, twig scraping twig, pine needles crunching, the hollow flap of an owl wing. He turned downstream, his hand cradling the pipe in his pocket as he absent-mindedly listened to the isolated layers of sound. For a moment he thought he heard a noise that sounded foreign to him, but whatever it was soon died away, and his mind fixed on the dam. Tomorrow he would start putting the logs in place. It was heavy work; he'd better get to bed soon. He'd go just a little farther, down to the clearing where old Prentiss used to have a shack. There would be moonlight there, spread like hovering breath over the open space.

He opened his eyes wide and flung out his arms, trying to take it all in. The next time he came here there might be snow covering everything — that too would be beautiful. Winter in the woods was . . . he hadn't the words to describe it to himself. You absorbed the cold and whiteness into your own body; it made you snap around, see the world new again, even though by February or March you were ready to scream at the bleakness. Every year it seemed to get harder to push through those long, raw final months.

Well, there were probably a few weeks of good weather left, and plenty of hard work ahead. Time to go to bed.

He had already turned back when he thought he heard the strange noise again. It seemed no more than a whisper carried on the wind from the woods. He paused, then walked slowly back across the field. Before long he was pretty sure he knew exactly where the sound was coming from.

Memories washed over him. That big rock ledge had been a favorite place through all his years up here — a retreat from the heat during summer, a cool place to go with a book.

He stopped a minute to light his pipe. Somebody had hung hemlock boughs off the ledge in a pathetic attempt to keep out bad weather. Pulling on his pipe, he waited to hear the sound again, but it didn't come, and after a few moments he hesitantly pushed one of the boughs aside and poked his head under the overhang. Blinking in the sudden darkness, it took him at least half a minute to see there was someone hunched up way back in the crevice where rock met earth. His glance took in the stove with a basket sitting on top of it. The body didn't move or make a sound and he cautiously backed out, causing the boughs to sway silently.

"Good God," he thought, "it must be the same girl!" He couldn't believe it. Yet, now that he saw her there, he realized it had been pretty odd, the way she kept coming back to the beech tree. It would

have been a long hike for somebody to make so often
— no matter how curious — all the way from the
village.

What was she doing here? How was she surviving? Didn't she have a family who worried about
her? Had she run away from home? She was like an
abandoned little animal curled up there in her dark
lair. How stupid to have put out that bread and
cheese for her the other day, encouraging her to stay!

Well, it still wasn't too late. There was no need to
get involved. Whoever she was, or why she was
here, wasn't his concern. Of course, he could — and
some would say he ought to — go in there and carry
her back to his place, give her a warm bed and a good
breakfast, then take her into town in the morning and
find out where she belonged. But had he ever behaved the way the world thought he should? There
was no reason to begin now. He vowed to himself
that if he saw her again near his place he'd tell her to
go home, get off his property.

Still — it was unbelievable! What would make this
girl — anybody — come up here and try to live like
that?

How many weeks had it been since he'd first seen
her? Three or four, anyway. Had she been staying
under the ledge all that time? Impossible! How had
she been feeding herself?

Anyway, it was sheer chance that she'd found this
particular place for a shelter. She could have gone to
some other part of the mountain and then he would
never have even known she existed. He was going

to walk away and leave her, just leave her, put one foot in front of the other, toward home.

By morning a cold fog had settled over the mountain, slipping into every low place. Sisul drew herself in under the blanket, chilly and miserable. To throw off the blanket and face a morning like this was too much, she thought. One bare leg pressed against the other. She pulled her shoulders down toward her knees like a toad.

More than just cold was keeping her in bed, however. Wasn't there something, a vague memory of a dream? Gluskabe standing silently outside her cave . . . A couple of weeks had passed since she'd felt him there, threatening her, yet there was something she had felt last night . . . Well, it was gone now; she couldn't catch it.

The morning was so cold, the raw edge of the day to come. It was going to get worse and worse as winter wore on. Could she stand this much longer? She told herself that if she stayed here she might get sick and die; people *did* die, after all — even children, even her mother.

What exactly was death, she wondered drowsily. Was it real, permanent? She saw a line in her mind — a rope, almost. Yes, a hemp rope, that divided the dead and the living. Could you cross back and forth, as if you were in a game of jump rope? Is that what Gluskabe did, and her mother?

Suddenly she was wide awake and hungry. She sat up, opened the oven door, and began stuffing dried berries into her mouth, then pulled the blanket tight around her shoulders and crawled out of the cave. Like a weak smile, the sun was insinuating its way into the fog. For a moment she sat and let its pale warmth fall on her. Her braids hung low and tangled in front of her. She pushed them back impatiently; ideas were taking shape.

First she was going to make a cape of birch bark. Uncomfortable or not, funny-looking or not, it would help to keep her warm and dry. Nothing else counted now. After that she would set about getting another blanket, maybe two.

By the next afternoon the coat was finished. Uneven, cracked at one shoulder, held together uncertainly with ground pine stems that would dry out in a day or so, it would nevertheless do for the moment. This was no time for perfection. Now she was on her way to the old man's place, around the back on the other side of the stream, making a path through a tangle of low brush. On her left she glimpsed the shack, went past it, then crept out to the edge of the bluff above the stream and looked down.

There was the *awenotc* below. She could see the top of his head, his white hair bouncing up and down as he pushed the wheelbarrow on which he'd balanced two heavy maple logs. Once again she found it hard to pull herself away. She could feel inside her own body the strain and effort of pushing the clumsy wheelbarrow over rocks and hillocks; then relief as the heavy logs slipped into their proper places. And when the man finally leaned back on his heels and regarded his work of the last fifteen minutes, she too experienced a sense of accomplishment. When he started off again with his empty barrow to load on more logs, she stealthily backed away from the edge of the bluff and ran to the rear of the shack, edged around, passed by the goat's pen, and slipped through the rough board doorway.

Emotion struck like a blow as soon as she stepped inside. Four months of a bleak, bareboned existence dropped into a gray void. Here in front of her was the simplest of enclosed spaces, a crude cabin room. Yet held within it, as in a tightly lidded attic trunk, were all the precious things: warmth, shadows and lights, surfaces that were soft or shiny or rough, smells, sounds. A board creaked; she could hear pitch dropping softly on the roof. What the sun sent down, that nameless something you could never touch — more than just light — was caught and held for a moment, making the whole place quiver with moving dust and glinting reflections. Here were cabinets with food and jars and dishes inside them, shelves laden with odd bits and pieces of stuff. There was a golden lamp with its knobs and crown to hold the glass chimney. There was a chair that rocked slightly when you moved toward it.

The shriveled remains of a match lying near the base of the kerosene lamp — what abundance of easy comfort it represented! A match had been struck, creating instant light and warmth, then was casually dropped and left to crumble away wherever it happened to fall.

The smell of the place: wood smoke, yeasty bread, pipe tobacco, wool work shirts, human sweat, together forming a cross-woven texture of a person's life.

She walked over to the bed, hearing her coat creak in the silence, and put out her hand to take the extra blanket folded neatly at the bottom. "Just for a moment," she whispered to herself, sitting on the soft edge of the bed. She lay back, the birch bark coat cracking beneath her. "No, no," she thought, "I mustn't. What if he walks in here and finds me?"

She jumped up, smoothed the quilt on the bed, and snatched up the blanket. On the way out her hand pulled back a little faded orange curtain; behind it were four loaves of bread, stacked side by side.

"Just one," she whispered. "Only take one." But her hand grabbed a second, and later, when she held the bread close to her and smelled it, she thought she had been crazy not to have taken all four.

VIII

November was here and the dam was almost finished. A thick bank of dry, porous earth had been dumped over the watertight core. Now Bruce was starting the outer shell of split logs, trying to fit them together so they would be as waterproof — he hoped — as the keel of a wooden ship.

The girl had gone. That was a relief. Sometimes he thought he saw a flicker of movement and would quickly glance toward the beech tree, but there was never anything there except a jay or a chickadee; that was all. A couple of weeks ago she had had the impudence to take a blanket off his bed and steal two loaves of bread. He had thought about going down to the rock ledge, giving her a piece of his mind, and taking the blanket back, but he kept putting it off — the days sped by; there was so much to do. Anyway, she must have left by now. Nights were down to around 20 degrees, pretty mild for November, but still cold enough to send anybody who wasn't an Eskimo scurrying back to civilization.

The day's work finished, he settled back comfortably on the rock and congratulated himself. He was going to make it after all! He was lucky: winter hadn't really set in yet; in two or three days the dam would be done.

He let his thoughts fly to next spring, to a vision of water lapping at the logs, the cleared lowland area covered over, the naked stumps hidden. Right there was where the Canada geese would land, water spraying high against their outstretched wings as they braked to a stop. He could hear them honking a wild cry in the dawn; could see himself leaping out of bed and running to watch them, his breath smoking in the cold air. Maybe two of them would stay and make a nest there under that bank . . .

Stop dreaming, he told himself. Geese won't land here the first spring, maybe not the second, the third — maybe not ever. Besides, why get so excited about a bunch of geese? What did they represent that was so important to him?

The sun was down; it was getting cold now. He looked up and noticed a thin fog closing in on the black rocks at the top of the mountain — like a restless ghost, he thought. A sudden wind blew the fog off, exposing the glistening peak. He slid off his perch and carried his tools up the hill, putting them carefully inside the shed and closing the door tight. It was going to be a bad night.

No snow was falling at bedtime, but a smell of raw dampness and a cutting, bitter wind foretold a storm. He slept fitfully, dreaming first of threatening, dark mountains and falling boulders, then of a dam made out of stacked-up wheelbarrows, which rusted and kept getting swept away by a torrential stream. A gust of wind was about to blow one of the wheelbarrows into his face when suddenly he awoke and was alive to the fact that a blizzard was screaming around the corners of the shack.

He jumped out of bed and ran to the window. His heart sank. Ah well, he thought, it could be worse. Tomorrow — if the storm ended by then — he could shovel the snow away and still get the dam finished. Maybe he'd be lucky. The ground under the snow wasn't frozen deep yet, and if the sun came out in the morning everything might turn to soup by noontime.

Back in bed, he started checking everything over: Selgie was safe and warm in her shed, along with the chickens. He hadn't gotten around to covering the woodpile with a tarpaulin yet — not serious. Tools were all put away, even the wheelbarrow, which he usually left propped up on the porch. Nothing out there the snow could hurt.

He turned on his side and tried to get back to sleep. For the first time in months, maybe a year, he found himself carried back to certain bleak, pitlike nights. How often he had lain sleepless on his slab in prison, his restless brain ranging over the sights and sounds that confronted him every day. The trembling play of firelight on the cabin ceiling forced its way into his consciousness. These were black thoughts, he told himself, and would only lead to blacker ones if he kept on.

He made his mind's eye range over the shack and yard and garden — they were all right; nothing there to worry about. Farther on his mind's eye went, down the embankment to the stream, the rock, now across the stream, on to the beech tree, the steep path down the mountain, down to Prentiss' old place, the meadow . . . finally to the opening under the rock ledge.

He knew he'd get there. There was no use hoping something else would intrude and say, "Here, it's me you want to think about, not that girl. She's left, Bruce; you know she must have."

The cabin felt chilly. He pulled himself out of bed again, poked at the fire, threw on some wood, and stood there barefooted, shivering in his underwear, watching the sparks flare and die. The wind was screaming more shrilly than before and he said out loud, "This is crazy, standing here in the middle of the night."

To save matches he often touched straws of wood to the fire when he needed a light. He watched a thin wood strip flare up in the dark; then he pushed back the glass of the kerosene lamp and lit the wick. A soft glow fell over everything — the maple rocking chair, a pile of books on the table, the rust-colored quilt on the bed — and seemed, for a moment, to quell the storm's ferocity. But he still heard the ominous tick-tick of snow driving hard against the windows. Giving a sigh, he walked behind the stove and pulled his heavy clothes off the peg.

Like a thousand tiny sword points, the icy snow hit his face as he slid down the embankment and leaped across the stream. But inside the woods the storm was softened, and for a moment he stood still and let everything swirl around him, losing himself in the thick-falling white stuff. What a wonder it all was! The first storm — here in the woods it was a feast, a deluge of goodness. Why sleep on such a night?

Once he left the protection of the woods the snow turned savage again, and the pain of the cold and ice brought involuntary tears to his eyes. He began to wonder seriously if he wasn't going mad, coming out on a night like this to rescue someone common sense told him wasn't there. It suddenly occurred to him that maybe he *wanted* her to be there. "Dear God," he thought, "am I so lonely that I'll battle a storm just on the chance of seeing a human face?"

The hemlock boughs that had hung so protectively

around the ledge the last time he had visited the cave were blowing straight out in the wind now. Before the night was over they would be torn away. A cascade of snow splashed over his cap as he half fell into the dark hole, and dazed by the storm, he lost his step completely, hitting his side against the edge of the stove.

He cried out softly. Trying to get his bearings in the confusion of snow and dark and the roar of wind was like being thrown blindfolded into a black night sea. He felt for the rock ledge, the stove.

Had he heard a sound? Was that a body huddled in the crevice?

"It's all right," he yelled through the wind. "You'll be all right now." Could there really be someone there?

In time his eyes accustomed themselves to the dark and he was able to make out the girl lying rigid against the rock, wrapped in a blanket — *his* blanket.

"Don't be afraid," he said, going toward her on his hands and knees.

He thought she shouted something and her eyes seemed to flash out of the darkness at him. "You'll be okay now!" he called. "Come on with me."

It looked as if she was trying to shrink farther back into the crevice. Her eyes did not stop glaring at him. His mittened hand reached for her.

"No! Leave me alone!" he heard her cry out.

Without thinking, he grabbed hold of her and managed to drag her into the open storm. She bit his hand and almost pulled away from him.

"Stop that!" he shouted. The snow drove angrily against them both. "What do you think I'm trying to do — hurt you? You'll freeze to death if you stay in that place tonight."

She didn't seem to hear him. Perhaps the storm had carried off his words. He had to fight with her to keep her from breaking away. Finally he managed to lift her up in his arms. She was heavy, but he was mad and determined now, and trudging on with her through the drifting snow, he had to hold her arms down so that she wouldn't hit him.

The snowy blankets fell off her when they stumbled into the shack, revealing in the yellow kerosene light a dirty, skinny girl wearing a filthy sweater that came down to her knees. Under the sweater was a white cotton dress, the same one he'd first seen her wearing months ago. Her legs were covered with scratches and bites which had gotten infected, had healed, and become infected again, leaving behind scars and broad brown marks. She gripped a hairbrush in her chapped hand.

He moved to push back the tangle that covered her face, but she backed away from him.

"I said I won't hurt you," he cried out. He was dizzy, almost sick, from the effort of carrying her up the embankment in knee-deep snow.

She still glowered at him. Again he thought of her as a cornered animal.

"All right." He shrugged and turned away. "I'll

leave you alone if that's what you want." Wearily he threw an armful of wood on the fire. "You can sleep in my bed. I'll sleep on the floor."

He was aware that she was standing in the middle of the cabin for a moment, making up her mind what to do next. He stood with his back to her and waited to see what would happen. What was he going to do if she ran out the door? Chase her? Tie her down? Impossible — he was so tired he could hardly stand up. If she left, that would be her business. He'd done all he could.

With relief, he heard her move to the bed.

In the quiet he heard again the click of snowflakes hitting against the glass of the cabin windows. He took some blankets off a shelf, put them down on the floor next to the stove, then sat down and began to unlace his boots. Reaching over to turn off the lamp, he glanced at her. She lay stiff on the bed, trembling.

"Why didn't you tell me you were cold?" He picked up a quilt and went over to her, but again she shrank away and looked at him with such stark fear that his heart was chilled.

"There's nothing to be afraid of. What terrible stories have they told you down in the village?"

She closed her eyes and turned away.

He leaned down and put the quilt next to her trembling body. Maybe it was wrong to leave her like that, but he couldn't do any more tonight. In the morning he'd be able to cope with her. Now he was too exhausted.

He turned off the kerosene lamp at last, stretched out on the floor, and, wondering briefly who she was and why she was living in a hole in the ground during a winter storm, he fell into a dead sleep.

IX

A pale morning light glimmered off the new snow,
filling the interior of the shack. Everything was still.
Sisul glanced over the ridges and valleys of the
patchwork quilt to the rough cabin walls. She ran
her finger back and forth over the soft cover.

How had this happened? There had been a face
peering down at her through the dark; the wind was
blowing; snow was beating into the cave. The white-
haired man! How had he known where she was?

The thought had come to her then, and again now, that somehow Gluskabe had finally arrived to help, just as her mother had promised. Or had he come to her as a hunter? Had it been so all along, that this man was really Gluskabe? Was this the next step in the old feeling she had of being pushed forward by some unknown force? Was the storm, the man speaking into her ear — Gluskabe, perhaps — part of the plan? No, she told herself, it was dangerous to think this way. He was just a man, an *awenotc*, not Gluskabe. He could do her harm. She must leave his cabin and go back to her cave.

But what good would that do? Now that he knew where she lived, wouldn't he come and get her again? She could move to a new place; find another cave. No, not in the snow. That was impossible. Even the thought was more than she could bear. What was left to her? She would have to beg — fight — whatever it took — somehow force him to leave her alone.

How could she? Whenever he asked her anything she was tongue-tied. She would never have the courage to talk to this stranger. How could she, Sisul, convince him of anything!

The only thing left to do was to slip out of bed, pull on her sweater and sneakers, pick up the blankets, and leave. Maybe if she just disappeared he would leave her alone.

From outside came shuffling noises, a low murmur. She sat up and saw that the floor by the stove where he had slept was bare. Now was her chance to get away. She leaped out of bed, grabbed her things, and opened the door.

Bruce stood facing her, a bucket of steaming goat's milk swinging from his hand. "You're up!" he exclaimed. "I'm going to fix pancakes." His pale gray eyes peered down at her for a moment; then he moved past and put the bucket by the sink.

He found himself wanting to be nice to her this morning. It was against his better judgment; but he felt dimly ashamed of last night; somehow he hadn't done enough. Now, almost against his will, he made up his mind to dig under that fear of hers.

He got on his knees and reached back into a cabinet under the sink. "There's some maple syrup left," he said as he grunted. First one arm, then two, disappeared under the sink. "I made it two years ago. You know, it takes forty gallons of sap to make one little gallon of syrup." Now his head was under the sink, too. "You have to boil and boil, day after day." Finally a bottle emerged, then his head. He handed the syrup to her and pushed himself off the floor.

He tried making conversation as he put the pancake batter together, as if it were not unusual for him to have someone with him. Ha — if she only knew the effort of getting out what sounded to his ears like so much gibberish! Or was she too hearing it that way? He began to feel that her silence was a rebuke.

"Now," he said expectantly, as they sat down at the table. He poured syrup over her pancakes for her.

Like cat and mouse they sat across from each other, each of them alert to the other, every sense awakened for a sign or move that would indicate the other's intention. Sisul found that to look up and meet this man's eyes was physically impossible, yet she was aware of every move he made. She told herself she should have left by now; that it was a mistake to let him give her breakfast. He might be trying to be nice, but that was only the surface, like the half-worn paint on her hairbrush. Soon he would say, "All right, let's go," and would try to force her back down to the village.

She ate slowly, her stomach rebelling at the rich food.

"Have you been under that ledge all fall?" he asked, watching her careful motions, taking note of the way her eyes stared down at her plate. "What'd you do for food?"

This time I will wait for an answer, he thought.

Sisul's silence was intensified by the sound of water falling from the eaves onto the cushion of snow outside. Her hands lay rigid at the sides of the plate, as if she were getting ready to push herself away from the table. "I managed," she finally murmured.

Bruce put down his fork and stood up, ostensibly to look for a pipe. He needed time to think. Before she'd wakened he'd been considering letting her stay for the morning while he worked on his chores. Then in the afternoon they would make the trip together down to the village. Now he saw that the thing to do was to get her out of here as soon as possible. She was an unpleasant, sullen brat. Last night she'd tried to bite him. Right after breakfast he was going to send her away, drag her down the whole damned mountain if he had to. His first instincts had been right. When he'd been a kid his mother had told him that all people had some good and bad in them, but over the years he'd never seen much good. It seemed as if the worst was always hiding there, ready to erupt in practically everybody he'd ever come across. Evidently this girl was no exception.

He strode back to the table. For an instant their eyes met. In that instant he thought he saw pain and fear and self-questioning. "Maybe her eyes mirror mine," he thought.

He groaned inwardly. What was happening? What was the matter with him? He was feeling things, having thoughts he couldn't have even imagined a day ago. He was afraid of himself, afraid that he might say something he didn't want to say, commit himself to something.

"I wasn't trying to interfere last night," he said, sitting down again. "I just didn't want you to freeze to death. My motives were no more sinister than that."

She looked up quickly. Interfere? Motives? Sinister? What was this *awenotc* talking about?

"The name is Bruce."

There was no response.

"You ought to tell me your name," he prompted. "It's the other half of the bargain."

"He mustn't know who I am," she thought. "Think up a name, fast!" Wild, unfocused things

84

raced through her mind, but no name came to her. It was no use.

"Okay, then I'll have to give you one." He pulled thoughtfully on his pipe. "I'll call you Aves." He pronounced it *Ah*-vehs.

Where had such an idea come from, he wondered. Why not call her Jane, or Liz? Why this fancy name?

"It means bird or birds, I think. Something like that. It's Latin."

She didn't respond, and continued sitting there stiffly.

Is there something wrong with her, he began to wonder. Can't she understand me? No, I bet she's rebellious, a half-out-of-control kid, full of anger toward herself and the world. Something like what I was like at that age. Kids like that can destroy everything around them. I'd better get rid of her fast.

"Where do you live when you're not camping out? I hope your parents know where you are."

The fire sizzled, and outside some jays called to each other over the snow. "My mother is dead," she murmured.

"Ah . . ." So that was it.

"Your father?"

She shrugged.

So, Bruce thought, there's no one. It looks as if she's run away — from where? He tried to remember if there was an orphanage nearby.

"Tell me . . ." He leaned forward. "What'd you live on down there? Where'd you get food?"

"There's plenty." She spoke slowly, barely above a whisper, and began to move her thumb across the grain of the table.

He sat back. "Go on," he said.

"There's food — in the field. There's *wapatoo* along the stream . . ."

His palm hit the table. "*Wapatoo!* What the hell is that?"

"A root. It's in the mud, under water. You boil it."

"Never! You never made a fire! I'd have seen the smoke."

"I was waiting for it to get cold."

For the first time he heard animation in her voice, and yes, there was a note of pride. "It got cold enough for you to steal a blanket."

She looked up sharply.

He shrugged. "I guess I didn't mind. Tell me, who taught you all this stuff about finding — what'd you call it? *Wapatoo?*"

"My mother. Before she died."

She said these words, as she had said everything, very simply and quietly, with a kind of measured space between the words, almost as if she were speaking a foreign language. Despite his caution, he found that her way of speaking touched him deeply, and as he studied her dirty thin face with its stubborn strong mouth and downcast eyes, he had to turn away.

"It's not easy to be confronted with this," he thought, "after sixteen years of solitude." Maybe anyone might have made such an impression on him after so long a time, but he had to fight a feeling that he ought to reach out to her.

After a moment he was able to turn back and look at her again. She must have had an Indian mother, white father, probably. A half-breed. He thought, "What am I going to do about her?"

"You said you had plenty of food. Did you really plan to stay there much longer?"

"Umm."

"Why, for God's sake?"

It was clear she wasn't going to answer.

He got up abruptly and began clearing the table. "I'll heat extra water so you can take a bath and wash your hair. You're filthy." Which old shirt could he give her, he wondered. That dress might as well be thrown out.

"I'm going to work on the dam now. Afterward we'll talk about what to do. Think about it while you clean yourself up."

She watched him pull on his jacket as he went out the door. He looked mad. Well, what did she care? Now was her chance to get away. She could climb upstream toward the top of the mountain. It was wild there; he'd never find her . . .

But that was crazy. Even if she made it, she would die up there. And anyway, did she have to? If she really put up a fight and wouldn't go, would he insist on taking her back to town? He couldn't carry her all the way down the mountain, could he?

If only she could get up enough courage to talk to him! Talk, Sisul; open your mouth! He said not to be afraid — maybe he meant it. Talk; explain that you only want to be left alone.

Slowly she pulled off her dress and ragged underwear and set to washing herself, flinching a little when the warm water touched her chapped skin. Could it be possible, she wondered again, that this man — Bruce, he said his name was — was Gluskabe in disguise? It was true; she supposed that she could have frozen last night. He had saved her. There was something about him that suggested a hidden force, like the hard rocks that lay under thin topsoil. Gluskabe was probably like that.

Well, she'd see. The test would soon come between her will and what she supposed was his determination to send her down the mountain.

Bruce discovered himself working on some words. Over the years this happened more and more often. Some mornings he'd wake up with something going through his head and it would take hold. Then he'd end up carrying the words around with him all day. Words — individual words — sometimes seemed like objects, tangible things he could feel and touch. He supposed it must have something to do with his never having anybody to talk to.

Now here he was, thinking about that name Aves ... She *did* remind me of a bird last night, he thought. She was like a dark bird; yes, a dark bird, huddled in her rock nest, cold snow blossoms tumbling down her face ... Ah, that sun feels good on my back. Won't last, though. More weather's coming in over the mountain.

What's going on? he wondered. All morning I've been saying things, thinking things that jump uncontrolled into my mind. "Aves," for God's sake. What could possibly have made him say that? Had his life become so barren that only slight contact with this girl was enough to push such a notion out of him — a word he couldn't even remember learning? For all he knew, it wasn't even Latin.

"Cut it out, Bruce," he said to himself. "You came down to the dam to get away from her. Use the time to clear your head."

What should he do? The prudent thing — he could hear a voice tapping it out in his mind — the prudent thing would be to take her down to the village and turn her over to the proper authorities.

A nice phrase, that: proper authorities!

What meaning did it have in the case of a girl whose parents were dead, who had run away from something so bad she was willing to hunt for roots in a stream and live in the ground wedged under a rock like a woodchuck?

Out of the corner of his eye he saw her coming down the embankment, a passing image of dark eyes and wet tussocks of hair. He saw her hesitate at the rock, then climb up, brush off the snow, and settle into the comfortable curve on top. Despite the sunshine, it was a cold November day. It occurred to him that she probably shouldn't be outside with a wet head. Wasn't that supposed to be unhealthy?

He stopped himself. What business was it of his whether she got sick! She didn't belong to him; he wasn't responsible for her. He gave a split log a final shove and kick, and waded past the rock to the wheelbarrow. She was gazing at the mountain — daydreaming, it looked like — and as he went by she let out a small cry. He must have startled her.

"You're so afraid all the time!" he exclaimed, reaching out to steady her. She stared down at him and he felt that she was questioning who he was. "Has somebody been beating you?" he demanded.

She backed off, slid down the rock, and ran up the hill into the shack.

Let her go, he said to himself, guiding the wheelbarrow along the rocky bank; just let her go. But wasn't this a good time to get it over with? Follow her, tell her to get her things together, and, if you must, pull her down the mountain. Better do it now before the afternoon wears on and it gets too dark.

When he came into the cabin he found her thrown across the bed, sobbing. He took a deep breath, then dragged a chair over, reached down, and touched her wet head. Time halted a moment. He was suddenly aware of dust dancing restlessly inside the light by the window.

She turned her head and looked up at him.

He put his hands on his knees. "I don't know what to do about you," he said. "Somebody's been treating you badly; you've been knocked around. Now you've run away. Is that right?"

She nodded.

"Where are your relatives? Who's supposed to take care of you?"

She shut her eyes and turned away.

"Come on, child," he said, not letting himself use that fancy name. "There must be somebody who wants you back. Somebody's probably looking for you. Worried sick. Maybe thinking you're dead. Where'd you live before you ran away?"

She remained silent. He began to pace back and forth between the stove and the bed. "I should explain something to you," he said. "I'm the hermit you've heard about. The crazy guy who lives on the mountain. I've done some bad things; had bad things happen to me. All I want to do with the years left to me is to live here. Live alone."

He lifted the big lid off the stove and began poking at the coals. "I don't want to have to bother with anybody. It's not you. I just don't like people. I've got to send you back to wherever you came from."

Sisul drew herself up on the bed. "Then I'll go back to my cave," she said. "That's my home. There's no place else."

Her brush lay on the pillow. She picked it up. "Don't worry — I promise I won't bother you," she added, and stood up.

"Wait a minute." He put his hand out to stop her.

She paused at the foot of the bed. Crying seemed to have shaken all the fear and uncertainty out of her; she now felt very strong. She watched him walk around, poking at things, sticking his hands in and out of his pants pockets. He went to a window, pulled out his pipe, and looked outside.

"I say to myself, why not? Why not let you go back there if you want to. That'll be the end of it and I won't have any more to do with you. But it's impossible. Last night's storm was like — nothing, nothing at all, a little spring shower — compared to what's coming. You've never been through a winter up here. At least" — he turned around and peered at her — "at least, I don't think you have, have you?"

This *awenotc* was definitely not Gluskabe, she decided. Gluskabe would never have had trouble making up his mind.

She shook her head. No, she'd never spent a winter on a mountainside before.

"One night the wind'll turn and start blowing from the southeast and all the snow will be driven right under that rock you call a cave and bury you alive. It could've happened last night. It doesn't matter how much food you have or how well you've planned. Nature doesn't give a damn for your planning. Sometimes I've thought this shack was going to be blown right off the mountain.

"It won't work, no matter how much you want it to. How could I sit up here, dry and comfortable, while you're down there in a hole in the ground, cold and eating roots, maybe freezing to death?"

"I'm not going anyplace but the cave," she insisted. "Maybe I can fix it up better so the snow can't get in. There's still time . . ."

"Dammit, that's crazy! Look out there — we're

going to have another storm tonight. See that gray stuff coming over the mountain?"

She knew he wasn't just making it up and trying to scare her. "I can't help it," she said, looking up at him. "I won't leave the cave. If you take me down the mountain I'll come right back again."

He turned away from her and stared at the wall. Could she really mean that she would rather die than go back to whatever it was she had run away from?

"Okay," he said quietly. "You'll have to stay here tonight. Tomorrow I'll help you get your cave fixed up."

Her heart pounded. She had won!

"I'm going down there now and make sure everything's all right." She threw him a quick look to see how he took this.

Few words were exchanged as he helped her improvise a pair of boots from pieces of leather and some rope. He made her put on a pair of his old pants, which he cut short to fit, and a wool shirt.

It was dusk when she returned. He'd half expected her not to — in a way he'd have been relieved if she hadn't. The waning sunlight had turned to an oily gold which reflected magnificently off her birch bark coat. She had decided to wear it with Wabanaki dignity.

Bruce did not laugh, and observed solemnly that he'd never seen anything so interesting since the night he'd dreamed Calvin Coolidge was running around in the rain in his long johns. Sisul hadn't the faintest idea of what he was talking about.

X

So began a permanent, if uneasy, arrangement.
Over the next few days the thickest logs from Bruce's
woodpile were hauled down and stacked in front of
the opening and around the sides of the cave. But
even with this better protection, if the weather
looked bad Bruce would pull on his heavy boots and
go down to the cave and insist on Sisul's staying with
him. Together they would tramp back to his place,
deepening a path through the high, growing white

banks. When the sky cleared or the temperature rose, Sisul would go back to her cave, usually loaded down with bread and canned goods.

Because Sisul was so silent, Bruce had no idea of how remote her inner life was from what they both thought of as the "real" world — that through her mind wended a mixture of half-believed Wabanaki myth and a vague acquaintance with contemporary life. Each time he saw her, though, he became more aware that she was imbued with pride, with determination, if need be, to stand alone, and with a spirit of oneness with the earth. It was obvious that she was very strong, very stubborn.

He was surprised to discover, one stormy evening, that she didn't know how to read. Several hours had passed, as they characteristically did, in complete silence.

Bruce got up from his chair, stretching and yawning. "Here, maybe you'd like to look at this," he said, handing her a book. "There's a poem about a night like tonight."

"I can't read," she mumbled.

"Can't — or don't?"

"Can't."

He sat back down, raised his eyebrows, and whistled softly — this was something!

"Didn't you go to school?" he asked, looking down at her.

"No," she said. She was sitting cross-legged on the floor by the stove, making a pair of mittens out of the cut-off part of the pants Bruce had given her.

He turned back to his book, rocking the chair lightly with his foot. After staring at the same paragraph for what seemed like ten minutes, he asked, "You want me to teach you to read?"

"No." She went on sewing. "I don't care about books."

He was more than half relieved by her answer. It was best to keep as much distance between them as possible.

As for Sisul, she was lying when she said she didn't care about books. It intrigued her that someone could sit for hours staring at print, turning pages, content to be silent. She had never seen anyone do that before. The Osborns never read, nor had her mother.

Her real reason for saying no was that she felt learning to read was a betrayal. A betrayal of what? Of an ironbound commitment to a way of life that might or might not exist! Although she couldn't admit it to herself, could not even dare to think such thoughts, it was a fact that she was beginning to doubt Gluskabe's reality. She was even beginning to doubt whether her mother still existed somewhere. Awatawessu had not come to her in some weeks; she had to remind herself to summon her. Days passed, she would forget, then suddenly remember, "Oh, yes, I should think about my mother."

During the next four months, beyond everything else, she was involved in winter — sheer, raw winter — and in doing what lovers of winter do. In the morning she would crawl out of the cave, sniff the day, then look around to see what had gone on while she'd been asleep. Days were her books; snow the pages on which night stories were written.

A taut net of prints laid down between the hiding places of his prey was a moment-by-moment account of a fox's adventures. A skittering tracery from bush to bush of the white-footed mouse, patterns woven alongside the stream by an otter in search of fish — all revealed tales of eager hunger, of long marches ending in the dead end of a snowbank, and sometimes of a bloody death.

One afternoon, just before sundown, Sisul happened on a family of deer drinking at a place in the stream where a fall of water kept ice from forming. She and the doe exchanged long looks. With silent dignity, the doe and her family slipped into the forest. Sisul followed their tracks and was led to a network of secret passageways between the low-hanging hemlock boughs. After this she spent afternoons sitting apart, watching the silent deer travel back and forth along their forest channels. They would nibble on hemlock lichen and stop sometimes to rest in a snowbank, leaving telltale oval bowls in the snow behind them.

The days lengthened and Sisul began to be awakened by the high shree of pine siskins. They, along with rusty-headed redpolls, came every morning in search of the few seeds that still held on. After storms she learned to listen for a chickadee's call over the sudden stillness and to watch one turn itself into a broom, brushing snow away from its feeding place.

Shapes of trees and stumps and rocks in thick white shrouds were transformed from day to day — sometimes from hour to hour — as blowing wind and melting sun became their sculptors.

She began to savor the sight of a single dead leaf, crisp against the sky, clinging to the extended hand of a black branch. She admired such a stubborn survivor.

Sometimes the smell of winter was too much for her, and she would lie down in the snow with her eyes closed and breathe until her senses ached.

When it snowed with thick, big flakes she would lean against a fallen log and let the flakes fall on her black hair. The snow wrapped her in silence; white was everywhere; white had turned into something alive — a breathing, animal thing. To be a snowflake, she thought, to take a long dizzy fall through the gray sky, to land on someone's black hair, then burst open . . .

She closed her eyes and leaned back against the log, letting her body seep into the winter earth, draining into whiteness. She tilted her face and let the flakes fall into her mouth; felt them sting her tongue. There was a brief bursting open, like a flower . . . and a memory of an afternoon of sun and color spent with her mother came to her. She'd been a young child then, and she and Awatawessu had been walking through a field of daisies. They'd walked on and on, the flowers grew thin and dry, and they came at last to a high field crested with blueberry bushes. They'd filled their baskets with berries, Awatawessu's brown fingers stripping the fruit quickly, Sisul's own hands working slowly. Sisul had put some berries into her mouth, letting the warm juice explode. She could almost taste them now as she lay in the snow . . . Deep inside her she felt as if a warm spring were coiling slowly out, reaching into her stomach and breast, up into her shoulders and arms, down through her legs. The snow was thick on her lashes and brow, water began to drip into her eyes, snow melted down her forehead . . .

For Sisul — now sometimes Aves — to step outside on a January afternoon was to throw open a past where layers of memories touched and melted into each other: winter, snow, blossom, flower, sun, Mother, berry, juice, snowflake.

For Bruce it was also a memorable winter. Nothing is different, he kept insisting to himself, and when Aves was not with him he told himself to forget about her, and set about his work and thoughts as he always had. Yet, he noticed with increasing annoyance, he was unusually preoccupied with the weather.

A wind would come up in the morning; throughout the day the temperature would drop, the sky darken. He would stick his head out the door every few hours, sniffing the air, debating with himself. With a sudden burst of decision, he would finally pull on his heavy clothing and tramp down to the cave. More often than not, she wasn't there. What did she do with herself all day, he wondered.

Ah, she was coming now; he could hear the snowshoes he'd made for her squeaking across the frozen snow. Slowly she would come into view through a haze of fir boughs, her ruddy face enveloped in a cloud of steam from her breath.

She never turned down his invitation to stay at the cabin until the weather cleared, but she never appeared eager to come, either. He always got a feeling of "All right, if you think it's best."

She was remarkably quiet, he thought, and thanked providence for that. A noisy, talkative kid would have been intolerable. As it was, he was thankful not to have to know too much about her. He didn't probe; she offered nothing. Yet he couldn't help being curious. She didn't know how to read, she'd said. But she certainly wasn't dumb, and she carried herself with what he thought of as Indian poise. Or was he imagining this? Wasn't he endowing her with characteristics he'd heard and read about all his life, characteristics that might be pure white man's fantasy, for all he knew?

It was best that she remained as she was: silent and unknown. When spring came, he would go down to the village — he'd need supplies by then anyway — and find out who she was and where she belonged. He certainly wasn't going to let her stay here forever.

Nevertheless, as winter progressed, certain things were revealed.

One day, as they struggled up the path together through a cruel afternoon storm, he shouted that the wind must be blowing about forty or fifty miles an hour.

"Yes," she said. "Wuchosen is beating his wing very hard." She had said the words without thinking. Probably he hadn't heard her above the wind, so it didn't matter.

But after supper that night he sat her down and asked her to tell him about "that wing thing" while he made some tea.

"It's not anything," she said, fiddling with a dead match.

Let it go, an inner voice told him. Another voice, more inner yet, urged him on. "You said it was something about the wind?"

"It's the Great Wind Bird," she said diffidently. "It's just an Indian story." She scraped at the match with her thumbnail.

"Yeah — and?"

"When it gets windy like this — my mother used to say it. It's nothing. Something about how he lives up north and sits on a rock at the end of the sky. Whenever he moves his wing the wind blows. That's all."

"Just one wing?" Bruce felt himself heading for a closeness he did not want, but he couldn't seem to stop. "That must be hard. Like moving one eyebrow." He demonstrated, holding an enamel cup in

101

each hand, moving one eyebrow up, the other down. "Why not both wings? Or does he save that for hurricanes?"

She laughed.

"Tell him," she heard her mother whisper. "It's time you let him know who you are."

"What if he makes fun of it?"

"Then you'll know."

Bruce sat down next to her, blowing on his tea.

Sisul said slowly, "You know who Gluskabe is?"

"Never heard of him."

"He's — a kind of god who does good things for Indians. He's not *the* god, like Jesus, but ..." she faltered. "I don't know exactly what he is, but he lived a long time ago and sometimes he comes back. My mother used to say he'd come back someday and make things better for us."

"By us," he interrupted, "you mean the Indians. Not white people."

She nodded, looking up at him. Had this made him mad?

"Well, come on," he urged. "Tell me about him, this Gluskabe. What's he have to do with the bird who only moves one wing?"

She took a deep breath, feeling her mother's voice rise inside her own.

"When Gluskabe was among men he used to go out in his canoe to kill sea birds. One day it grew very windy, then it got worse. Finally he couldn't go out in his canoe at all; it was a storm. And he said to himself, 'Wuchosen the Wind Bird has done this.'

102

"So he went to find Wuchosen, a great white bird sitting on his high rock.

" 'Grandfather,' Gluskabe said, 'you have caused this wind and storm; it is too much. Be easier with your wings!'

"But Wuchosen answered, 'I've been here a long time and I'll move my wings any way I please. So go away and don't bother me.'

"Gluskabe got very mad and rose up in a cloud. From up there he was able to grab Wuchosen like a duck, and that's what he did. Wuchosen squealed and wiggled, but Gluskabe had a good hold on him. He tied his wings to his body and threw him down in a crack between some rocks and left him there.

"Now Gluskabe could go out in his canoe any time he liked, the water was so quiet. But as weeks and months went by with no wind, the water began to smell bad and get thick with weeds. Soon Gluskabe couldn't even paddle his canoe. So he went back to the crack where he'd thrown Wuchosen and pulled him out. He sat him back on his high rock and untied one of his wings. That's why we say 'Wuchosen is moving his wing' when we feel the wind blowing."

Bruce put his cup down and began filling his pipe. "I liked that a lot," he finally said. "You know any more?"

"Umm," she murmured, sipping her tea.

"Will you tell me some? Are they Iroquois? Algonquin?"

"I'm a Wabanaki," she said.

103

"Never heard of 'em," he said, getting up. "Where'd you come from? Out west somewhere?"

"No, up north. Maine."

"Maine! So Gluskabe was out in the ocean chasing sea birds off the coast of Maine!" He sounded excited. "Were you ever there yourself?"

"I think so."

"You remember anything about it?"

"Not really, just . . ."

"Just what?"

"Just . . . there was sun on the water, and an old woman with wrinkled hands. That's all . . . I don't know." She shook her head.

Bruce said, "It's all blurry and vague, but still you can feel it, right?"

She nodded.

He lit his pipe and stretched out. "Come on, tell me more. How'd you get from Maine to New Hampshire?"

"We walked, I guess. It's the same. Blurry. Just roads and trucks."

"And — ?"

"My mother got some work." She paused. "Then she died last summer."

Was she telling him too much? It was tempting to spill it all out. Could it be that he really wanted to listen? No, she'd better watch out. This might be a trick to get her to tell him who she really was.

"And then you ran away? What made you come up here?"

She paused, then shrugged.

"You don't want to tell me any more."

"No." She looked down at her feet.

"Okay," he said, shrugging his own shoulders to let her know it didn't matter. He picked up a book and began to read.

XI

The winter was not all glory for Sisul. Although the cave was warm now because she dared to keep a fire going through the night and could heat stones to warm her feet on, the fire raced through fuel like hungry men at a feast, and most of her day was spent in dragging dead limbs from longer and longer distances. With snow covering the ground, there was no more wild food available. Dismayed, she watched her stored-up treasure slowly diminish into smaller and smaller piles. She saw that without Bruce's handouts of food and logs and warm clothing she could not have survived.

Sometimes it was so cold outside she couldn't make herself get up, and would spend the morning, half asleep, wrapped in blankets next to the weak fire. By noon she might stick her head out the entrance, shiver as the cold wind hit, and pull back in, like a mole shunning daylight. Eventually she would crawl outside, still drowsy from the effects of the close air, and force herself to hunt for more wood. She began to hate wind, the cold, the whole icy mountainside — not only hate them, but fear them in a way that made her shrivel up inside. She began to get stomachaches that grew worse and lasted longer as one cold, bitter day ran into another.

Then, strung out like jewels, a week of sunny, crackling mornings would come along, and once again winter was something she wanted to throw herself into and be part of.

To go to Bruce's place on bad days was always a temptation, but she clenched her fists and vowed not to go. It was all right if he invited her, but she was not going to let herself ask him. More and more she worried about what he was going to do when spring came. Wouldn't he go down the mountain and ask people about her?

It was hard to understand him. He wasn't cruel, like Walter Osborn. Nor was he constantly smiling and trying to please, like Mr. Finch. Although he was strong and courageous, as she imagined Gluskabe to be, she felt there was something missing. Sometimes he was too open, willing to admit that he didn't always know what to do and that he could make mistakes; she considered this a weakness. Her mother never hesitated over a decision — neither did Walter Osborn, for that matter. It was as if Bruce couldn't make up his mind about her.

Often he showed impatience when she refused to answer his questions, and sometimes he'd say, "Dammit, I'd like to give you a good shaking when you act this way. What's the matter with you — did I ever do anything to make you behave like this?"

But most of the time he scarcely talked to her, as if he didn't want to be bothered by her. Once he yelled at her. Selgie escaped one afternoon and wandered off. Bruce assumed Sisul had carelessly left Selgie's door open, and told her so.

"Don't ever go near Selgie's shed again, understand?" he lashed out.

"I never do," was all she could say. She stomped off home, infuriated. How could he think she would do such a thing!

The next day he came down to the cave and said he was sorry. He hadn't noticed until later, but the shed latch had gotten worn and he guessed that was how it had happened.

Sisul felt a combination of rage and disgust. It was bad enough that he'd accused her unjustly, but it was worse to hear him apologize. Strong people didn't make mistakes.

"Did Selgie come back?" she asked grudgingly.

"Umm. Just before sundown."

Despite these feelings, she found to her shame that she really did want to reveal more of herself to him. The night she had told him about Wuchosen stood out as a rare, special moment in her life. It was the first time she had ever talked openly to anyone besides Awatawessu, and for the first time she experienced the exhilaration of letting herself be known to someone who was half a stranger. She waited for him to ask her to tell him another story. But he never did.

Not until February was half over did they exchange any real words again, and the cause of it was accidental.

One overcast, raw day Sisul discovered that her hairbrush was missing. She tramped back and forth over tracks through the woods, hoping at every new turn to see it lying half buried in the snow. As the gray afternoon shadows grew long, she couldn't tell any longer what she was seeing, and when she arrived at the cabin she was reaching the end of her self-control.

Bruce opened the door. He didn't seem pleased to see her.

"Come in. I'm just cleaning that thing." He gestured toward a shotgun lying across the table.

"Did you see my hairbrush?" she asked, her eyes scanning the room.

"Lost it? Well, you'll manage. You never brush your hair anyway." He sat down and picked up the gun.

109

"What did Indians use to brush their hair with?" he asked. "They didn't have fancy hairbrushes like that."

"Combs made out of wood," she mumbled, and started looking under the chair and bed, around the woodpile, behind the stove. The girl with the sunbonnet was lying somewhere in the snow, she was thinking. Even if it was found now, the picture would be ruined. She was on the verge of crying.

"This cleaning is a stupid thing I do every six months or so," Bruce was saying. "I never use this thing."

She didn't hear him; she was turning up one side, then the other, of the mattress.

"I don't like guns," he said, clearing his throat. "They stir up bad instincts."

She was only half listening. "Instincts?"

"Kind of deep hidden needs. You don't have much control over them. Like being hungry . . ."

Her eyes ranged over the shelves for a last look. Deep hidden needs . . . what about secret longings for a sunny garden and ruffled dresses? Was that an instinct? Something you didn't have much control over . . .

She moved toward the door.

"Too bad you lost it," he said, putting the gun back on the wall. "But you'll fix something up; it's not a great tragedy . . ."

"I know." She rushed out the door, almost sobbing.

The next morning she was poking morosely at the fire when Bruce suddenly appeared at the entrance to the cave. "Listen," he said, crawling in past the fire and settling himself next to her. "I've got to tell you about what happened. I don't want you being scared of me, worrying about what I might do with that gun."

He cleared his throat uneasily. "I don't even use it for hunting. I got hold of it when I first came up here, thinking I would need it — for what, I don't know — maybe for shooting bears, or some damn fool thing. I shouldn't even have a gun. I'd get into trouble if they ever found out."

"If who found out?" she asked.

"Ex-cons aren't allowed to have guns," he said bluntly. "Especially if they were sent up for armed robbery."

She didn't seem to understand. Was it possible that she didn't know about him?

"Don't you know who I am?" he finally asked.

"Just what you told me. Somebody who wants to be left alone. A hermit, you said."

"I was in prison. Don't tell me you didn't know that."

"Prison?" Prison was where they put murderers, thieves, bad men. Her mother used to say Walter Osborn should be shut up in prison.

"I thought everybody down in the village knew at least that much about me."

"I didn't know anybody was here — not until

I heard you chopping down trees one day."

He took off his mitten and rubbed his cheek. "You get crazy ideas, living alone." He gave a wry laugh. "Got anything to eat? What about that *wapatoo* stuff?"

She leaned back, reached into the oven, and pulled out some dried apple. "The *wapatoo*'s all gone."

"What's bad about prison," he said, chewing slowly, "is that it puts a fast end to dreams. Good dreams, I mean. It's hard to believe in — well, much of anything — after fourteen years in prison."

He fiddled impatiently with the stove while he waited for her to respond. Doesn't he ever notice how hard it is for me to find something to say? Sisul wondered.

"Is *anybody* good?" she finally asked. What was really going through her head was the thought that all *awenotcwak* must be bad. Even this one had been put in prison!

"Well, what about it?" he asked her. "You're not a bad person, are you? Have you ever been mean to anybody? Done anybody real harm?"

"No."

"Do you think you could, though? Is it in you to hurt, maybe to want somebody — well, if not dead, at least not around?"

She immediately thought of Walter Osborn, then of the rabbit. She hadn't wanted the rabbit to die; that at least she was sure of. Yet she had killed him. As for Walter . . . "I guess so," she murmured.

"There you are," he said with a sigh. "That's what I meant before, about instincts. I'm not saying we're born with it, but it's there, all right. Even you know it. I guess everybody does."

They were silent; only the sound of the fire's muffled cracking filled the cave.

"Maybe that's not fair," he said after a while. "Maybe not everybody's like that. Maybe if you've always had everything good, everybody nice to you all the time . . . I don't know . . . What was it like, where you came from? What did they do to you?"

She shrugged.

"Did you get hit, punished a lot?"

"A little. It was mostly my mother."

"Your mother hit you?"

"Oh, no! He hit *her*."

"He? Who's he? What kind of a place was this?"

She shifted her legs and poked at the fire.

"Come on, Aves, you've got to tell somebody about it sometime. I'd never make you go back to a place like that." He hardly noticed he'd called her Aves just now. He'd been trying to avoid calling her anything at all, but when they were talking like this, Aves seemed perfectly natural. He'd been thinking of her as Aves all along, he realized.

He was beginning to convince her. Still, she knew she must hold back from telling him everything. If he *really* knew who the Osborns were . . . And could she trust an *awenotc*, especially one who'd been in prison? It was getting cold out. She got up and

113

brought a blanket — *his* blanket — over. "My mother went to work at — this place," she said, pulling the blanket around her shoulders. "We came in nineteen twenty-seven, when I was about five. There was an old lady and her brother, and my mother kept the house clean and did all the work. The brother stayed away a lot; then he used to come home in the middle of the night. My mother usually kept me away from him as much as she could, but I could hear him. He was drunk."

"Why did your mother stay in a place like that?" he asked after a while. "Couldn't she get work anyplace else?"

"I guess not," she answered slowly. "There's the Depression. And she was sick. We would've gone back to Maine if she wasn't sick."

"Was she sick a long while?"

"She had the coughing sickness. It wasn't so bad at first."

TB, he said to himself. "Did anybody get a doctor for her?"

"No."

He sighed. "Those people, that woman and her brother — they don't have any kind of a claim on you, do they?"

She looked at him as if she didn't understand.

"I mean, they don't have any legal hold over you or anything. They're just people your mother worked for, right?"

"Umm," she said. She was preoccupied with peeling bark off a stick.

"You don't have any relatives? No aunts or uncles?"

Her heart skipped a beat. Could he have guessed something?

"Maybe ... maybe in Wachussami," she said hurriedly.

"Where the hell's that?"

"Up in Maine. I told you; where we come from."

"So as far as you know for sure, you have nobody in the world?"

"That's right," she said, averting her eyes.

XII

Aves — Sisul — she no longer knew what to call herself. She was kneeling in the meadow, digging up dandelions. For the next few days a thready little crown would lie buried at the center of a ring of ragged new leaves. Then — did it happen overnight? — the crown would push itself up, wave jauntily at the end of a stem, and one bright morning open itself to the air, a golden flower. All the new growth — russet leaves and tight-packed flower kernel — was good to eat. Delicious, in fact. The roots were good, too, once you peeled off the skin. It was painstaking work, pulling the whole plant out of the thick dirt without snapping the root off.

But to be out getting food again — that was wonderful. Not that the last two months hadn't flown by. If she had thought about it in advance, she might have imagined that February and March would drag by, the long tails of winter. But no, a sense of inevitable, slow, meticulous change hung in the air, filling the outdoors with compressed excitement. Late in January came a thaw, which sent Bruce out with taps and tin cans up and down the stream, hammering little hollowed-out elderberry twigs into all the sugar maples. Depending on how fast the sap ran, there might be long days filled with tending the big fire, crunching over snow, carrying brimming cans toward the smell of wood smoke, pouring the watery sap into the steaming iron kettle. Sisul never said, "Can I help?" and Bruce never asked her to; but gradually she fell into working with him, sometimes side by side. Their understanding was silent.

Toward the middle of March, Bruce began to worry about the dam's cracking under the pressure of ice pushing from behind. Every morning and afternoon he went down and broke up the ice with an ax. Sometimes Sisul helped. Leaning to rest on his ax, she asked, "When will the geese come?"

She was thinking of what her mother used to say — that in spring the first small flock of geese went north as scouts. If they came back, then the others

117

took wing, carrying all the small birds on their backs. This was why, Awatawessu had said, songbirds suddenly appeared the day after geese had been heard going north.

"Maybe in a week or so," Bruce answered. "When the real March thaw comes. Maybe not until April. Hard to say . . .

"They probably won't stop here, though," he added.

"What if they do?"

"I suppose they'll just stop, feed, then go on. A couple might stay and make a nest, raise their young."

"Is that what you want?"

"Ahuh."

"Where do they go?"

"Up north."

"To Maine?"

"I guess so. Canada. Way up."

They had chopped enough ice, and sat down, panting, on the rock.

"Have you seen those places?" she asked him.

He hit his boot against the rock, knocking off some snow. "No. Someday, maybe. For some reason I think I'd like to end my days up there. As if it would make any difference . . ."

"As if what would make any difference?"

"Where I die."

"Oh." She sat with her mittened hands in her lap, looking at the ashen sky. "What happens when you die?"

He could hardly hear the words, she held them back so.

I could pretend I wasn't listening, he thought.

". . . What happens? I don't know. People say that spirits, souls, live on somewhere."

"In the sky?"

He shrugged.

"Do you believe that?" she asked.

"I guess not. Are you thinking of your mother?"

She nodded. "You keep saying you don't know."

He looked away. Down the mountain a heavy mist hung across the valley, settling on the tops of the trees. In the absence of sunlight the pine trees looked black and unyielding; petrified, almost. "I think when we die, we die. Before we're born there's nothing; after we die there's nothing."

She shook her head. "You're wrong."

"How do you know?"

"Sometimes my mother comes to me," she said flatly.

He looked at her. She was examining her mittens. "You can see her and touch her?"

"Yes."

He rubbed his nose thoughtfully, then asked her if she'd stay for supper.

Sisul thought about that conversation many times in the next weeks. Bruce had said there was nothing after death. His statement, coupled with the fact, which she had not told him, that her mother no longer *did* appear, but seemed to be a memory only

— something to be thought about and remembered, not a living, independent being — scared her. Maybe it was true that when you died it was the end. It didn't seem fair, somehow. Why let you live at all if that was the way it was to be?

Meanwhile her life — her own life — was not, as it had been, one continuous thread of day-to-day happenings experienced at the moment, then forgotten about. Or, if not forgotten, at least never considered or pondered. Since she had run away from the Osborns she was beginning to think of events of the past as something quite separate and distinct from the present. Whatever lay in the future was more separate yet. Memories and sensations of the past, like dead greenery lying under the snow, might come back to color and shape the present, but nevertheless, they were past, gone, never to be lived again. The continuing presence of her mother, which had been the touchstone of her existence until the last few months, was receding into the background, and she had new preoccupations.

She knelt in the field thinking vaguely about all these things as she dug the early dandelions. March had come and gone, April was starting, and no geese had stopped. Separately — she at her cave, Bruce at the cabin — they had heard them honking high overhead in early mornings and twilights. Bruce had said nothing about it; she never spoke of it either. She remembered, though, how Bruce had said they were going up north where he thought he'd like to die. She couldn't help wondering how much he thought about that. It was true he was pretty old. Did everybody start thinking that way when they got old?

Wet dirt stuck to her hands and she felt an itch on her head. Leaning back, she peered into the gray skies while she rubbed her hand slowly back and forth over the cold grass. Her hand was clean now, but her head no longer itched. The sky was low today; a raw wind was coming up; bare trees began to rub against one another . . . and what was that flash of red down at the bottom of the field?

Her hands flew involuntarily to her head as if to protect it from a blow. Something moved at the foot of the field, camouflaged, except for a red hunting cap, against the russet April forest.

Still surrounding her was the patch of dandelions, but when she looked down it seemed to rise up like an ocean, and through a screen of sickening green came a figure moving steadily toward her.

Close now, the man's small fox eyes burned a hole through the sea of dandelions. How long had he been standing at the edge of the forest, breathing and watching?

"So this is where you been hiding," a voice drawled through the wavering wall. "Crazy kid — what'd you want to run away for?"

In a minute his heavy boot would kick the basket and grind the newly dug plants into the dirt. Lean forward, she told herself, pick up the basket, think about washing the plants in the stream, about how the icy water will push back the leaves and stems, seeking out the hidden dirt.

"Poor Sisul, what a way to spend the winter! Well, you won't have to stay with that crazy guy anymore. You can come back home. I'm not mad at you or anything."

... Rise up slowly, slink back into the underbrush, get on the wrong side of the wind ... It's an old trick; everyone knows a fox will pretend to be just a friendly visitor — he may even smile! Don't let him see that you know his eyes and ears and nose are waiting to signal the moment to rush in and kill. Move slowly and drift away, drift away ...

His smell curled around her: liquor and stale tobacco. "Hey now, you're not afraid of me, are you?"

Rough leather near enough to touch, to push away. Simultaneously he rushed in and she grabbed the knife, the basket fell and dandelions spilled over the ground.

"Come home with me!" he demanded, and twisted her wrist until the knife fell.

There was still time to resist, to turn and pull while he put his hand over her mouth, to sink her teeth into the palm of his hand.

Listen! There was screaming: her own voice.

"Shut up, you damned Indian brat." He spat out the words and hit her on the side of her head. She felt herself fall in a heap in the grass, tried to scramble away, but he grabbed her and lifted her up, this time holding her mouth closed, his thumb digging into her chin.

More shouting, but now it wasn't her voice. There

was Bruce, running toward them, yelling and waving his gun over his head. "Leave her alone!" The shouting flew across the raw air. "Damn you! Leave her alone!"

She felt her hand come to rest on a heavy, mud-packed boot. She pounded on the leather as if she could force it to move.

"I didn't know your land went down this far," Walter drawled, casually kicking her hand away.

"By God, I'll shoot you dead if you touch that girl again!" Bruce's words flew off in the wind, and his mouth seemed to open and shut mechanically, as if he had lost control over it. "Come over here, Aves!" he finally screamed.

She ran to him and was now able to look back. Walter's red hunting cap had fallen off. He leaned down to pick it up.

One year ago she had watched him bend over a pool of blood on the floor of the kitchen. Beside the blood, her hair wetted and curled by it, lay her mother. "You've killed her," whispered Miss Osborn, picking nervously at the raw skin on her hands.

"I didn't do that; she coughed it up. Besides, she's not dead," Walter had said, and moved away. "Get Sisul to clean up the mess and get her into bed."

"Shouldn't we call the doctor?"

"What for? She'll die anyway." He had laughed, swept a pack of cigarettes off the shelf, and walked out, slamming the back door.

He was laughing now. "Aves, is it," he said, put-

123

ting the hat back on. "Who told you that? Her name is Sisul. Sisul Osborn. When'd you change your name, honey?" He ambled toward them.

"Stay down there." Bruce waved the gun again. "Who the hell are you? What are you doing here?"

"I came to get my niece." Walter pointed toward her. "It's about time she came home. Eight months is a long time to be away from your folks, ain't it, Sisul?" He stepped forward again, arms extended, ready to take her.

"Get away." Bruce pointed the gun at Osborn's chest. "What folks?"

"Her aunt and uncle. I'm her Uncle Walter."

"Is that true?" Bruce demanded of Sisul in a strangled murmur.

"Yes," she told him, and saw his mouth tighten.

"How do I know who you are?" he shouted. "You could be a homicidal maniac, for all I know. Get the hell off my property."

Walter saluted and took a step backward. "That's not gonna work, mister. Try to keep her if you want, but I'll have the police up here by supper time. That girl's my brother's daughter. I'm her nearest relative."

He let this sink in, then came forward again. "Why not just hand her over now? Get your things, Sisul. I'll wait here for you."

"Get off my property." Bruce moved toward him. "Right now."

"Okay, okay." Osborn took a few more steps down the slope. "Not bad for a — what was that old story?

A botched-up B 'n' E job? Some kind of crook, anyhow. It's your funeral. See you later with the police. Sisul, you be ready to leave, oh, around eight o'clock." He went off, sticking his hands in his pockets, whistling.

Bruce turned wearily and looked down. "Why in God's name didn't you tell me?"

"You'd have made me go back," she whispered.

He left her sitting on the ground, went down the hill, and carefully put the dandelions back in the basket. It took him a long time, and as he walked up toward her she tried to read in his eyes what her fate would be. When she reached out and took the basket he grabbed her hand.

"We'll have to get out of here," he said. He began pulling her up the hill. "We've only got — " he looked at his watch " — less than six hours."

"You don't have to go with me," she kept saying, sobbing. "I'll go somewhere by myself."

Bruce acted as if he hadn't heard her; he just went on packing and fastening things down in the cabin. The last thing he did, after turning Selgie loose, was to board up the windows and doors.

XIII

"**W**here you headed?" An old man stuck his weatherbeaten head out the high window of a truck.

"North," Bruce yelled up to him.

"I ain't goin' far but you'll put a few miles on. Climb in — throw your gear in back there."

He was all bone and gristle, this fellow, his pale eyes bleached by more than a half century of squinting into the sun.

"Smoke?" he asked, once Bruce and Sisul were

settled on the torn leather seats. He thrust a mangled pack of Camels in front of Bruce.

"Thanks, I've got my pipe here somewhere," Bruce said, poking around for his tobacco pouch. He was not altogether surprised to discover that his hands were shaking. Not so easy to throw yourself into life again after so many years.

The man tussled with the stick shift. "Damned gears."

After a fierce struggle, he got the truck into first, and they lurched forward. The truck was coaxed into second, then third, and, with a final protest from beneath the floorboards, it began humming along at thirty miles an hour.

Bruce gazed out at the landscape unfolding before him, tried to breathe more easily, and to watch the hillsides of spring woods and fields pass by in the late afternoon light as if this were something that happened to him every day.

"You from around here?"

"No — Massachusetts." Bruce gave Sisul a poke with his elbow.

"Thought you sounded like an out-of-stater. Goin' down to Quoddy, are you."

"No . . ."

The man laughed, displaying a mouthful of long yellow teeth. "That'll make you the first, then. I guess you're a little old for that. Must be pretty rough work. Every young fellow I pick up all this spring — they're all bound for Quoddy. They're puttin' up a town, schools, stores, everything.

You watch; they'll overdo it. Always do."

He paused and whistled to himself, resting his elbow on the open window.

"Nice to see spring again," Bruce offered.

"Wasn't too bad a winter. Seen lots worse. Yep, those fellows ought to read the papers before they go chasin' all the way down to Quoddy. You wait; it'll get strangled in the birthin' just like the Triple A. Saved us last year, but it gave me a catch to see all those potatoes rottin' ... thousands starvin' to death ..."

It was hard to follow what the old man was talking about. What was Quoddy? The Triple A? What were the "its" and "theys" scattered through this man's talk? Bruce finally gave up. Pounding through his brain was the conviction that he had been thrust into something irreversible and disastrous.

No one had made him go with the girl. In fact, he had debated with himself even while he was packing to leave, seeing his choice very clearly. So he couldn't blame it on impulse. On one side there was his plan to live out his life alone. It took tangible shape before his mind's eye as he sat bouncing rhythmically in the deep-springed seat, half hearing the monotony of the old man's voice. He saw his life as a solitary human — sixteen years — suspended above him like a beautiful crystal, magical in its simplicity, its bright purity.

He could still reach out and clasp it, hold it in his hand. It was not too late. It was all he had, this life he'd created for himself; wasn't it like committing suicide to let himself be parted from it? "Give the girl whatever she needs for a long trip," he said to himself. "Food, money, warm clothing — say good-by and turn back." He fought down an impulse to jump out of the truck.

"Better than havin' to give up, though," the voice droned on beside him. "You work your life out over a piece of land and then they foreclose on you. Never thought I'd . . ."

Bruce's ear picked up the key word. The old man. would think something was funny if he didn't speak up now and then. Here was something he thought he could talk about. He'd heard talk down at Finch's store on his yearly trips for supplies. "Many farms around here foreclosed?"

"Enough to make a man cry." He pointed down the road, off to the right. "Look over there — ain't that a pathetic sight? John Prout's place."

They gazed on a ruined farmhouse sagging behind tall rusty weeds. Light fell on the roof in such a way that bald places glistened where the shingles had blown off. Bruce caught himself admiring it. It was beautiful in its way; it contained a special kind of melancholy. He shook himself. What was wrong with him! That house represented misery, hunger. You didn't go around mooning over how pretty it looked!

"Foreclosure?"

"Hell yes," the old man said. "And he only had three years to go . . ."

"What's he do now?"

"God knows. First thing, Sally — that was his wife — she got sick in the flu epidemic and died; maybe it was a blessin'." He gave Bruce a quick look. "That's a black thought, ain't it?" he said quietly.

"I told him he should stick around, maybe things'd turn better, but he said no and took off. Don't know where he went. We keep lookin' for him to turn up someday; maybe we'll get a letter. He was here like us, twenty years. Neighbors, you might say. Don't stand thinkin' about ... Hey, look at that, will you!" The truck came to an uncertain halt, then moaningly backed up.

Bruce's heart leaped. Police? A roadblock? "What's the matter?" he cried.

"Didn't you see that?" The truck pulled to a stop next to a ditch by a field of grazing cows. It was a peaceful enough scene, but the old fellow jumped out of the truck as if his life depended on it.

"One a those Guernseys got loose," he shouted back over his shoulder. "Fence is broke back along there. Be back in a minute."

Bruce and Sisul climbed out after him. Before they could catch up, the old man was already at work on the cow — pushing, yelling at her, slapping her rump.

"Heyyup! Come on, Bossy, heyyup!" He alternately coaxed and browbeat.

Bruce took off his jacket, flapped it when the cow started in his direction. Then Sisul dashed in, yelling, feeling her sneakers sink into the soft field dirt.

130

At last the cow seemed to comprehend, and suddenly turned and trotted docilely toward the rest of the herd.

"Dumb stubborn beasts." The old man laughed as they walked back through the tall grass to the truck. A covey of partridge was startled and flew off into the late afternoon light.

Bruce laughed too. For a fleeting moment he felt himself filled with a wonderful happiness. Suddenly it felt good to be out in the world again. The panic he'd felt only a few moments before was replaced by an exhilaration he'd never known before. By God, he should have gotten himself off that mountain long ago — he needed the world; he needed people. He gave Sisul a boost up into the truck and jumped in after her, pulling the door shut.

"It's a helluva life," the man said, swinging himself into the driver's seat. "That farm's run by old lady Schaeffer," he went on when they were moving again. "She's pushin' eighty, I'd say. That fence's been broke all year. Guess I'll have to get over here and fix it, now that grazin' time is back."

Dusk was falling, the truck windows were closed, and the old man's voice rolled on like the endless countryside itself. A low, pale light picked out the new growth, still red and yellow against the browns of the aging hillsides.

"Course it's always been tough here, dontcha know . . . My kids went off a coupla years back . . . Oregon, lumberin', another one on the bum . . ."

"I don't have kids I can talk about," Bruce was

thinking. "In fact, there isn't much I *can* talk about down here . . ." He looked at Sisul, who was sitting rigidly beside him. "She must feel pretty uncertain about her future," he thought. "I never have been able to figure out what goes on in that Wabanaki head of hers. *That's* something I ought to give a little thought to."

"If you ain't goin' to Quoddy, where you goin'?"

The man cleared his throat and repeated the question a little louder. ". . . if you don't mind my askin'," he added.

"Sorry, guess I dozed off," Bruce said, coming to. "This girl here — she comes from Maine. I'm taking her back home."

Sisul looked up at Bruce. He hoped the old man didn't notice her look of startled surprise.

"She yours?" the man asked.

"No."

"I see . . ." He pulled thoughtfully on his nose. "Never been down to Maine myself. It's poorer than poor, that's all I know. Potatoes and rocks; that's all they got. Where exactly you goin'?"

Bruce said the first thing that popped into his head. "Penobscot Bay."

"Don't know it myself. Been there before?"

"No . . ."

"Well, here's where I turn off." Abruptly, the truck pulled to a stop by a dirt road. The man hopped out and came around and opened the door. While Bruce reached around to get their gear from the back he saw him take Sisul off and talk to her.

"So long," Bruce called, hopping off the running board. "Thanks a lot."

They shook hands. "Lightens the day to have somebody to talk to," the man said. His eyes looked off for a moment to the ramshackle farm at the end of the road. "Keeps you from thinkin' too much when it don't do no good.

"So long," he waved, and with a mighty shifting of gears, turned down the road.

Bruce looked at Sisul.

"What did he say to you?"

"He asked me if everything was all right and if there was anything I wanted to tell him."

"Suspicious old codger! What'd you say?"

"I told him everything was fine. Then he said he was sorry if he cussed a lot. He said he wasn't used to having young ladies around."

They laughed and watched the dust swell behind the truck, then die in the ebbing light. From far off came the wail of a train whistle.

"Are you really going with me to Maine?" she asked.

"I can't think of anyplace else to go, can you?"

XIV

New England had stayed the same, Bruce thought. Even here, where the B & M Railroad cut through forest and fields. The trains rushed past — slices of civilization, tiny windows lit up yellow — there was a roar, some smoke, an occasional can of garbage dumped out the rear of a dining car. Peepers and tree toads might pause — it was hard to tell with the noise — but the mink and fox, busy at their night work, never even looked up.

Settling down under their blankets near the tracks, Bruce and Sisul worked over their thoughts as they turned their backs against the cold open sky.

Sisul felt as if she were still being swept along by the green wave that had washed over her when Walter Osborn walked out of the woods. Now the water was receding, pulling her along with it. It wasn't an altogether unpleasant feeling, being swept along by events this way. Deep down, hadn't she known that something would have to happen — if not today, tomorrow; if not this month, then next? Walter had to find her someday; she had to leave the mountain someday. All in all, it might be for the best. Soon she would be in Wachussami, where she would find her Indian past.

There was no doubting Bruce anymore. She could trust him. Looking back, she saw that they had been trusting each other for some time now. She couldn't even imagine how the winter would have been without him. She would have died. Now that it was over, she could admit that to herself.

Would Bruce have really used that gun, she wondered. Maybe that was what he was thinking about right now. He was so silent. He'd hardly spoken to her since they'd left the old man and the truck. Yet for a while, back by the farm, when they'd chased the cow, he'd seemed happier than she'd ever seen him before. For a moment she'd dared to hope that he didn't mind leaving the mountain.

Once long ago she'd promised she wouldn't be a bother to him. And although she'd meant it when she'd said he didn't have to leave with her now, she had to confess she was glad not to be alone. But she *was* being a bother. She had to figure out a way to make that up. He even said he'd take her all the way to Maine!

She turned over and looked at the sky. Up there, bright, just where it ought to be at this time of year, was what she'd heard Bruce call the Big Dipper. But her mother said there was really a Bear up there. Now, in spring, the Bear was climbing out of its den toward the north. Creeping up on it were the seven bird hunters. Can I still remember them, she asked herself. Much had passed since she had heard her mother's voice telling the story of the hunters who pursued the Bear through spring and summer, until finally he was attacked outside his den in the autumn, his drops of blood falling on earth, making the leaves turn red.

Sisul felt herself reaching back into the dark chamber of her childhood. The names for the seven stars — there they stood, each word suspended above her: Robin, Chickadee — dragging her pot to catch the bear grease — then Moosebird, Pigeon, Blue Jay . . . or was it Owl who came next? She began again, counting with her fingers under the blanket: Robin, Chickadee, Moosebird . . . and now she heard her mother's voice coming down from the north sky, saying the words in her careful, deep voice: "Robin, Chickadee . . ." With a deep rush Sisul gave herself up to her mother, feeling the encirclement of her arms and a sinking softness that meant yes, comfort, warm, love, tenderness, heartbeat, no evil . . . She stirred only slightly when a long freight train rattled by at midnight.

At midnight Bruce was still awake. He felt swept along too, but he, Bruce, was doing the sweeping. "What have I done," he asked himself over and over.

Despite his resolve to begin again down here in the real world — "facing life," he guessed people would call it — and despite his real concern over Aves, he couldn't help thinking about the beautiful crystal that represented life on the mountain to him. In his imagination he could still reach out and touch it. Lying underneath it was a dark, formless mass that stretched into a shapeless future.

"Come on, Bruce; stop dramatizing this," he said to himself. He'd help Aves — Sisul — he'd better get used to calling her that — he'd help her find her Indian relatives. (Funny, now that he was able to admit that Aves signified something special to him, the name was being taken away.) Then he could go back to the mountain. It was as simple as that. Only a matter of a week or so; that was all. What was a week or two in a lifetime?

. . . Would he have used that gun this afternoon? It was a black tendril of a thought he kept pushing away . . . One thing he knew. Whether he needed it for food or not, he had no business with a gun. As soon as he got back to the mountain he was going to throw it into the stream.

His thoughts began to fragment, as they will at four o'clock in the morning, and he saw before him an image of Aves making her way down the embankment, with Walter and the police in pursuit. "No, I couldn't have made any other choice," he thought.

Sure, if he wanted to see it one way, there was the simplicity, the ease — the beautiful crystal — of living alone. But there were new things to see and feel, a whole new world to catch up with. Beyond that, there was a young girl to get to know. "I've been running away from her," he said to himself. "And now that she must leave me, I must try very hard to do what's best for *her*. Not *me*, anymore."

He turned over and looked up at the stars. Look, there was the Big Dipper, as bright here as it was over the mountain: some verities would always remain. It felt good to be away; invigorating. It all proved he should have broken out long ago.

The peepers went on magically chanting; he began listening to them instead of to his own thoughts. Finally, just before dawn, he thought he fell asleep, but he wasn't sure.

"I was thinking last night," Bruce said as they hopped up and down, warming themselves over a little fire. "About a lot of things. Too many, maybe. But what's most important now is to get you to Wachussami. It's not very smart to take a direct route. We'd better stick to side roads. What do you think — will your uncle try to follow us?"

Sisul was braiding her hair. "I don't know. Maybe."

"How much does he care — that's what I'm asking.

Why does he want you back so much?"

She too had asked herself this. "Maybe he wants to get back what he thinks he owns," she said.

Bruce nodded. "Seems a funny reason." He rubbed his hands over the fire. "Well, we'll stick to the roads that twist around — and not take any more rides for a couple of days."

At lunch time they got a map from a gas station and sat under a tree, eating Selgie's cheese and Bruce's bread. Bruce propped the map up on his knees.

"Damned if I can find it," he said after a while. "It would help if you knew how to read. I could be looking right at it and not seeing it."

"What?"

"Wachussami. I can't find it."

Sisul gazed at the ground, rubbing her hand over the stiff new growth. "If you write it out for me, I can look for the same letters . . ."

He looked hard at her, remembering how she had rebuffed him when he'd wanted to teach her to read during the winter. He wrote WACHUSSAMI on the edge of the map. "It must be something like that. Maybe one *s* and two *m*'s."

So that's how it looks, she thought.

WACHUSSAMI.

Those two curves in the middle — what were they? she asked.

The *s*'s, Bruce said. He spelled out the whole word for her, saying the letters and pointing at them with his finger.

She stared at the word, then closed her eyes and

tried to hold it in her mind. For her, it was a cipher signifying much more than a few scrawled lines on the side of a map. It seemed to contain, like a seed, other words that themselves were bursting with more words yet, all filled with feelings that had no name, or none that she knew. Wachussami meant Mother, Gluskabe, rocks, sunlight, fleeting shadows, a sense of time that went back, back . . .

But could those pencil lines really stand for all that? Other people reading the same letters wouldn't have these feelings. They'd mean something quite different — perhaps almost nothing — to them. To Bruce, for instance, the word *Wachussami* would mean only: the place I have to take Aves. That was all. And to her mother the word must have meant a whole busy, living world, figured with definite people, full of corners and shadows, tiny worlds within the bigger one. Her mother must have known which trees in Wachussami had limbs for climbing, and where the anthills lay, and what the smells of certain rooms were.

What of the other words on this map? Did each of them hold thoughts and secrets for the people who knew them? Was everyone walking around with a head full of his own private world? For her, Sisul, the words *cave in the woods* were openings into sensations and images only she — no one else — could touch.

There was near magic in this white man's way of putting words into scrawled signs. It meant that other people, strangers, could learn a word that, in a way, belonged to someone else. And if those strangers could not know and feel the word as you did, could you bring them closer to it by the use of more and more words? If you wanted to. Perhaps you might keep certain words secret, only your own.

Her eyes scanned the map, picking out the scattered, countless names.

"Could you say some of them to me?" she asked. She bent over the map and pointed to a word.

"That's Portland. Look, right at the foot of this bay." Bruce's finger traced around the arch of Casco Bay. "All those are islands — like so many rocks thrown out to sea."

She looked up, puzzled.

Bruce leaned over, ruffling his hair. "I'll bet Indians made maps — like this."

In the soft dirt under the tree he made a dot. "That's my cabin," he said. Then he drew a snake line for the stream, making it bulge as it passed by the field, and made another dot for her cave. Farther off appeared another snake and beyond it a circle. "That's the creek and the town."

They bent again over the paper map, and Bruce's finger moved from the ocean to the little patches of blue, which were lakes, to the blue veins, which were rivers, and to the black dots, which meant towns sitting on the yellow, which stood for land.

"Say the names," she murmured, and so the yeasty, nearly edible place names of Maine began rolling off his tongue — Allagash, Aroostook, Androscoggin, Damariscotta, Smyrna, Wytoplitlock, Eggemoggin

141

Reach, Lake Umbagog, Mattamiscontis, Meduxne-keag, Kennebunkport, ending with the king of them all, Mooselookmeguntic — and she repeated them faster and faster, until the tide of sounds overtook them and they began to laugh helplessly, stretched out in the grass, the map flung aside.

They never found Wachussami, though, and Bruce said it might be too small a place to put on a map.

The afternoon was sunny and the dirt road was gentle under their feet. Although their mood was light — lightness seemed to be in the air itself — it seemed important to talk about serious things.

Bruce stopped to fuss with his pipe. "What was it like at the Osborns'?"

"They — were mean."

"You've told me that before. What happened?"

"I didn't always see. I could hear Walter come home in the middle of the night. At first it was always quiet and I would lie in bed waiting. Then I'd hear him shout at my mother's door and my mother yell. She would cough. Sometimes I tried to go to her, but she would never let me in . . ."

Bruce's hand brushed her shoulder. "Never mind. Tell me about the sister. She couldn't have been so bad."

Sisul scoffed. "She would come out to the kitchen in the morning and say things like 'Be sure you never touch my dishes, Sisul.' We had to use different things from her. She didn't want our hands to touch anything she was going to touch. We could never use the bathroom. We had to use the privy outside and get our water from the well for washing ourselves. She thought we were dirty. We — disgusted her."

"But didn't you tell me your mother was there as a housekeeper? How could she keep from touching things?"

"We did the hard work — the floors, the windows, the laundry, shoveling coal. But nothing to do with food. She didn't want to put anything into her mouth that we'd touched."

Bruce groaned to himself. It hurt to hear this. He remembered his own first feelings toward her; how anxious he'd been to get her out of his shack, off "his" mountain.

He pulled himself together and asked Sisul what she knew about her father. "I guess he was Walter's brother," he said.

"All I know is that he got killed in a lumbering accident when we lived in Maine. My mother told me he was a happy man; that she loved him very much."

"Do you remember him at all?"

Sisul shook her head.

"You never saw a picture or anything — a wedding picture? Did your mother ever show you anything — a piece of paper that said they were married?"

"No . . ."

"Are you sure — did anyone ever say anything to you about this — was your mother married to your father?"

"Oh, yes."

"Why I'm asking — it's just, if they weren't married, then the Osborns wouldn't have any claim on you. Not legally, anyway."

"Then I'd be illegitimate."

Bruce sucked in his breath. "Where in God's name did you hear that word?"

"Miss Osborn. That's what she kept telling my mother I was. My mother would say, 'You're crazy. Sisul is your niece.'"

Bruce said, "I believe your mother. She wouldn't have left Maine and gone to the Osborns if she hadn't been married. By the way, what was your father's name?"

"Len."

"Len Osborn. Okay, I guess I know all you have to tell me. No, wait a minute. While we're on the subject of names, what do you want me to call you? I guess I'd better learn to say Sisul. I've been putting it off, if you want to know the truth. I like Aves. It's — well, it's come to mean something to me." He studied her reaction.

Sisul found it hard to answer. She forced herself to look steadily into his eyes and finally said, "I guess Aves means something to me, too. As if you think I'm special. But Sisul's — well," she said, "it's me."

Bruce smiled. "We're being stupid," he said. "What really matters is that you *are* special. What difference does your name make? Tell you what. I'll try to get used to calling you Sisul, especially since we're going back to Wachussami. But maybe

I'll still think of you as Aves. And I know damned well I'll forget lots of times and make a mistake. I'll try my best.

"Now one other thing. Promise me you're not holding anything back this time. I understand why you did it up on the mountain. Maybe you were right, for all I know. But I can't see any reason to do it now."

"If I remember anything else, I'll tell you." She looked at him very seriously as she said this, and he believed her.

"Okay. Now all I have to do is find out where in blazes Wachussami is."

XV

Passing through villages and towns in the days that followed, they began to feel more and more as if they were moving through an unreal landscape. Not that the Main Streets they walked and browsed in weren't ordinary. To Bruce, in some ways they were as familiar as his own skin.

But no idyllic place of Sisul's hairbrush fantasy was this land of gas stations and ice-cream stands, of Kozee Kabins and auto junkyards, of peeling billboards and shiny five-and-ten-cent stores. Sisul hardly knew what to make of it and kept asking herself what it all meant. Where was something strong and lasting, something she could understand and trust?

First her eyes took in only storefronts and signs. She spent long minutes gazing at jewelry and cosmetics in store windows and at pasted-up enlargements of smooth-faced women and men on the movie theaters. Is that how it really is, she wondered, studying the pictures of Jean Harlow and John Barrymore kissing on a white couch, of Rogers and Astaire dancing under rows of sparkling chandeliers, their hair and clothes touched by a soft, heaven-sent light.

Then she began to pay attention to people on the streets, and stared solemnly at their workaday faces, wondering what lay behind them. What went on in their heads? What were they feeling? Did she have anything in common with them? She tried to listen in on conversations, and caught fragments here and there. But she never heard anything beyond the commonplaces she'd heard at Finch's store.

Where were the connections between all these things? Was the glitter on display as real as the everyday plainness? Did ordinary people somewhere — behind the wooden doors of their houses, perhaps — deck themselves in jewels and dance under rows of sparkling lamps? Was the glitter a kind of background to life that everyone but her knew about and accepted as the ordinary way of things?

Her mother's way of looking at it — that everything

not of the Indian world was white man's junk —
didn't satisfy her. It never had, though it did occur to
her that one strong blow of wind could carry all these
signs and pictures and even the storefronts away,
much as she used to imagine her own breath blowing
away the people who lived in the radio tubes in Mr.
Finch's store.

But there was too much of it. You couldn't blow it
all away. People crowded together, cars stopped at
traffic lights, office buildings — sights she saw even
in the small towns were dizzying to her. She had
thought that Maine was a place she could walk
around in a day or so; that it belonged to Indians.
Now, as she traced her progress over the yellow map
from town to town and river to river, she began to
understand how huge the *awenotcwak*'s world was.
Yet her mother had said it had all belonged to Indians once.

She felt relieved whenever they left the streets behind. Entering the open countryside felt like stepping into a cool bath. More than ever she knew that
woodlands and mountains, streams and empty fields,
belonged to her like her own breath. Maybe she
would never understand how towns and cities
worked. She knew instinctively that if she did, it
would mean killing something in her. She couldn't
be open to both.

They decided to head for the coast. Bruce said that
whether Wachussami was there or not, he wanted to
get a look at the sea and islands, and she agreed. She

had never seen the ocean, at least not that she could remember.

That night they saw a fire blazing by some railroad tracks. Walking over to see what was going on, they found themselves among seven or eight men gathered around the fire.

"Mind if we join you for a while?" Bruce asked. "If we could just heat up some food."

"Help yourself," somebody said.

Bruce learned about hoboes that night, listening to the men talk about riding the rails, picking up work here and there. It looked to him as if there must be bad trouble all over.

He murmured to Sisul, "It's funny. I hear these guys talk and can't help thinking that the world back then — when I went up to the mountain — maybe it wasn't so bad. Times were easier then. Maybe if I'd stuck with it . . ."

"But they put you in prison. Isn't that why you had to go to the mountain?"

"Nobody *made* me. I wanted to go. In a way you're right, though. I needed to be on the mountain. It's come to mean everything to me."

Sisul held down the question she'd wanted to ask Bruce for some time. She silently watched the hoboes settling down by the fire. Finally she burst out with it. "Why did they make you go to prison? Did you kill somebody?" She tried to read his face by the firelight. She thought she saw pain there.

He rubbed his cheek. "My God, have you been thinking that about me all this time? No, Sisul, I did not. Why didn't you ask before?"

"I was afraid you'd get mad at me."

"You're right. I probably would have. Not anymore, though. I'm going to tell you about it right now."

He described the attempted robbery to her; then the time he'd spent in prison. "All those wasted years," he concluded. "I spent a long time making up for one moment of stupidity when I let myself get talked into carrying a gun and holding up a store."

Sisul ran her fingers through some pine needles. "It's hard to believe. You — you're not like that."

"I guess that's the nicest thing I've ever had said to me," Bruce murmured. "Maybe that means I've changed."

"But —" Sisul hesitated.

"Go on," he said.

"You were going to shoot Walter."

Bruce shook his head. "No, Sisul. I'll never know for sure, but I'm almost certain I only wanted to scare him.

"I know this, though. There are times when a gun seems like an easy answer. I'm not going to let myself be tempted. Not ever again."

"How can you stop being tempted?" she asked.

"That's easy. Throw the gun away. Maybe I'll bury it behind a log in the dam. A fitting end, don't you think?"

He leaned over and passed his hand over her hair.

"As usual, your hair could use a little attention. That reminds me. Did you ever find your brush?"

Sisul shook her head. "I haven't thought about it for a long while."

"Why was it so special, anyway?"

Sisul studied the fire. "I'm not so sure anymore. It was so pretty ..." That must sound silly, she thought.

"I can understand that," Bruce said. "Probably neither of us ever had many pretty things.

"We had the mountain though," he added.

Early in the morning Sisul had a dream. Awatawessu appeared, smiling and beautiful, her black hair sailing back in the wind like the leaves of willow trees in March. She moved to Sisul, then passed beyond her, smiling in the wind, smiling. Sisul tried to catch her, to hold her for a moment. But it was no use. Awatawessu only moved smilingly past. "She's going up north," Sisul later remembered thinking to herself. "She's going to Maine and she's smiling because I'm coming too."

When Sisul awakened she was so happy she could hardly contain her eager anticipation. Soon she'd be in her rightful home!

Continuing their walk toward the sea that morning Bruce began to notice more details of the new world he'd been thrust into. In the old days, even in the middle of most towns, you could usually hear birds and insects, the wind blowing through a tree. The countryside was never completely obliterated. Now only a few horse-drawn milk carts were left. Instead there were billboards announcing the splendors of Frigidaires, Van Raalte silk gloves, Lucky Strikes, Bond Bread, Milky Ways, Four Roses whiskey, a movie called *King Kong*.

Then for the first time, in Portland, they saw soup lines: young men and women along with the old, shuffling forward, waiting to be fed. Down by the waterfront were rows of shanties and tumble-down shacks. People had even made shelters out of cardboard and tin cans. Old people looked sick and kids ran 'round half naked, sores on their bodies, no shoes, the fire of hunger staring out of their eyes. "No silk gloves here," Bruce thought.

"So this is what it's really like," Sisul thought. Surely the girls she saw here had no pretty little houses with hollyhocks to return to, no pretty dresses in closets.

Sisul looked up at Bruce. "You look sad," she said.

"I guess I am. Those kids' eyes almost spoke."

"Umm," Sisul said. "It makes me think of my mother."

"Did she — did she look like that?"

Sisul nodded.

Bruce grasped her shoulder. "I'm sorry. I didn't even think about what you might be feeling."

That afternoon Bruce made his first gesture to a new world. After they'd passed the third ice-cream place in a little seaside town he grabbed Sisul and said, "Come on. You need some cheering up."

Sisul's eyes shone as they stepped inside a store
that advertised silver dishes of sundaes with strawberries running down the slopes of vanilla ice cream,
whipped cream showering the strawberries, walnuts,
and a single red cherry sitting on top, king of the
mountain. Behind the counter stood a girl whose
cupid's-bow mouth was outlined with shiny lipstick.
On the wall behind her was a sign that said: FLAVORS
— CHOC VAN STRA COF PCH.

"What's P-C-H?" Bruce asked.

The girl looked at him blankly.

"In back of you; it says P-C-H. What's that?"

She turned and studied the sign.

"Oh. Peach," she said. "That's peach. We're all
out. We only got vanilla and strawberry left."

"That's VAN and STRA?"

She looked at him as if she thought he was insane.

"We'll take two of each," he said.

"You want *four*?"

"No," Bruce reconsidered. "I'll tell you what. Put
two scoops on each cone. Two cones, four scoops.
Can you do that?"

She paused and said quietly, "What you want is
doubles."

Sisul watched the girl closely as she proceeded to
take the metal covers off the ice cream and dig in
with her scoop. Steam rose from the dark holes. After pushing the balls of vanilla deep into the cones,
the girl dipped the scoop into a bowl of milky water,
then took off another lid and dug out the strawberry,

153

her arm plunging in deeper this time.

"You'd think she'd never seen ice cream before," the girl said, looking at Sisul.

"Yes, wouldn't you," Bruce said dryly.

"That's six for a double, twelve for two," the girl said.

Outside they found a tree to sit under. Bruce got down to the bottom of his cone first.

"This little end," he said, holding the tip of the cone in his fingers. "On my street there was an old man who used to give all the kids money for cones on the first day of summer every year. There was a store next to the river by the railroad station, and after we'd eaten our cones down to here, we'd throw them into the water and watch the fish rise to get them."

"Here's mine," Sisul said, holding up the end of her cone.

They leaned over an iron-railed bridge on the way out of town and threw the cone ends into the stream that ran lazily by. If there were fish down there, it was impossible to see them in the muddy water. As they watched the cone ends float downstream, Bruce felt a sudden ache of nostalgia wash over him.

"Why am I crying?" he thought. "For myself? Do I pity myself so much?" No, it wasn't for his own life that he wept, but for what might have been for everyone, for all the abandoned dreams.

When the sea dances in bright light off the coast of Maine, it is a sight that makes everyone — Gluskabe himself — catch his breath. The colors are gaudy: orange cliffs, green sea, the sky an order of blue that makes one want to embrace it and keep it forever inside. You stand and stare and smell and listen to the gulls screaming through the wind, to the sound of seas drenching over the rocks — and you reach out. If only there were something to touch, to carry home!

You put your hand in the water: it is so cold your fingers ache. You pick up a shell, ten shells, fifty shells, each one demanding notice. This one is lustrous in the sun; this one has a perfect form; this one has a shape you've never seen before; this one is a special shade of yellow; this one is whiter than any of the rest; this one is translucent; and look, here is a dried starfish, and scattered here are bleached sea cucumbers, all perfect, and sand dollars — hadn't you noticed them before? You wash the sand off them — it is strangely pleasant to feel the ache of the icy water now — how far away are Arctic icebergs, you wonder.

Later you go over them one at a time, still able to see each one as it was. You pour water over them and they shine again, but you must face facts: they are dead things now, beginning to smell bad. Perhaps you will dry them in the sun and carry them away in a basket, but more likely you will dump them back on the sand. There really is no way to keep the sea with you.

In fact, its memory dims over the months. Sometimes you recall best the foggy days when everything you touched was cold and damp, even your own skin. The foghorns always began at night, and, waking up, you thought, "How beautiful, how mournful they are." But by midafternoon of the next day you thought, "They are driving me crazy." You walked down to the sea but you couldn't even see the water hitting the cliffs. There was only a menacing hiss somewhere in the smoke below.

But when you return, months, years later, you stand on the cliff and see the shifting luminous greens and the blue that is too real, and once again everything that matters is sky and sea and rock.

XVI

A rocky shore pocketed with sand inlets. Behind, spruce trees are black spires. The sky, blue; the sun, hot. Gulls are wheeling above two lone figures against the rocks. For a long time the figures do not move or talk to each other. Then one, the smaller of the two, stretches out. She turns over on her stomach and watches a hermit crab labor in his tidal pool.

The other figure moves, but only a hand or a foot.

He feels he is thinking something profound, but in reality his mind is blank. He is a rock, riven by wind and heat.

He shifts a leg. Man must eat.

"We ought to collect driftwood for a fire."

Words don't belong. Did he say them out loud?

Sisul breaks off a small black shell from a rock. "What's this?" she shouts, holding it up for him to see.

"Something to eat. Get all you can. I'll get the wood."

But he doesn't move. Stone can't move. Slowly he puts his hands against the warm rock and pushes. He is up. He moves. He is independent, a man after all.

Stiff at first, he's finally able to leap from rock to rock like a boy, until he reaches a high bluff.

He looks back at the girl kneeling at the stone face, pulling off mussels. Her face is brown as the rocks; her black hair flies in the wind. Her mouth is set and serious.

"Sisul," he shouts. "I care; I care about you very much." She looks up, waves, and smiles. The wind carries his words out to sea.

It was dark. The fire had burned high, making sparks in the wind, but now was fallen low. Their stomachs were full.

"I almost remember things," she said, leaning back. The cliff at her back was still warm. "In the afternoon when I was sitting on that rock I thought,

'I've been here before.' Something flashed through me."

"You remember any people?" Bruce asked, yawning. The sea wind had made him sleepy.

"Just a story. A sort of funny old story. I think Mother first told it to me when we came to the sea one day."

"Tell me. Does it have a name?"

"Gluskabe and the Whale."

"Old Gluskabe again. Is he in every story?"

"When I first saw you I thought maybe you were him," she said.

"Really?" Bruce sat up. "Good Lord, what a responsibility! To be Gluskabe, creator of the Wabanakis!"

"Don't make fun." She laughed in spite of herself.

"No," he protested, "I wish I *had* been Gluskabe. I'm sorry I'm not. I'd have done well by you. I'd have pushed those mean white men right back in the sea, back where they belonged. No mercy."

"But then there wouldn't have been you."

"What do you mean? I'm Gluskabe!"

"No. You're Bruce," she said matter-of-factly.

"White."

"Yes."

"Do you mind that?"

"I don't notice anymore."

Neither spoke for a moment as they listened to the surf washing in. Bruce leaned back against the cliff. "Now tell me about old Glubey and the Whale," he said.

159

"Gluskabe lived alone on an island for seven years, and when the time came to leave, he took his dogs and went to the shore and looked far out to sea over the waves and sang the magic song that whales obey. Sure enough, there came a large whale, and she carried him well and easily over toward the mainland. But she was afraid of getting into shallow water, or of running ashore, and Gluskabe wanted her to go on so he wouldn't have to get his feet wet. So when she asked him if he saw land he lied and said, 'No.'

"So she went on. But when she saw shells below and the water growing shallow she said, 'Does not the land show itself like a bowstring?' and Gluskabe said, 'Oh, no. We're still very far from land.'

"Then the water grew so shallow that she heard the song of the clams as they lay under the sand. The clams were telling her to throw Gluskabe off and let him drown. For these clams were Gluskabe's deadly enemies. The whale didn't understand clam language, though, and asked Gluskabe what they were saying. He answered her this way:

> They tell you to hurry, to hurry,
> To hurry Gluskabe along
> Over the water
> Away as fast as you can!

"Then the whale went like lightning and suddenly found herself high on the shore. She cried out:

> Alas, my grandchild,
> You have been my death.

I can never leave the land.
I shall swim in the sea no more.

"But Gluskabe sang back to her:

Have no fear, Noogumee,
You shall not suffer.
You will swim in the sea once more.

"Then with a push of his bow against her head he sent the whale off into deep water.

"As she left she said, 'You haven't anything such as an old pipe and some tobacco?'

"'Oh, yes,' Gluskabe said, 'you want tobacco. Hmm, let me see.'

"So he gave her a short pipe and tobacco and even a light. And the whale, now in good spirits, sailed away, smoking as she went, while Gluskabe, standing silent on the shore and leaning on his maple bow, saw the long low cloud that followed her until she vanished in the far away."

"Will you tell me a new story every night?" Bruce said. "Until they run out?"

"All right."

"Sisul." His tone changed. "I don't know how to say this, though I've thought a lot about it. How Indian are you? You know what I mean. What do you believe, really?"

"I can't tell you," she said uncertainly.

"Why not?"

"Maybe — because I don't know."

"What worries me is . . . the world isn't Indian

anymore, Sisul. Even for Indians."

"Part of it is!" she protested. "Wait till we get to Wachussami."

A pang went through him. She *did* believe.

"How is it going to be different from any other town in Maine with an Indian name?"

"Because there are Indians there — my mother's people. Of course it will be different!"

She said no more, and pulled herself and her blanket into a protected bay in the rocks. He could see her sitting there, her elbows on her drawn-up knees, staring out at the stars.

He stretched out, listening to the quiet night sounds of the sea. Something had made him shout out those words, *I care about you,* this afternoon. The funny thing was, saying it didn't seem to make him feel any different about Sisul, but very different about himself. He, Bruce, had said that this girl was special to him, which meant that he, Bruce, was capable of feeling something strong and positive about a separate person.

What did it mean, to love? He'd once read that the test of love was caring more about the person you loved than about yourself. Wasn't the ultimate test of caring the willingness to die for that person? What if Sisul were going to be run over by a car tomorrow and he could save her only by getting killed himself? Would he do it? Tomorrow, right away in the morning? He laughed at himself. He had no idea what he would do, any more than he had known that he was going to shout out those words.

So — he felt something for this girl: a desire to reach out to her, to help her, to make sure she was taken care of. More, he wanted to know her mind, find out what was going on in there, how she saw the world. That, as best as he could tell, was what he felt.

No, there was more to it than that. He realized that he was deeply grateful to this girl for having pulled him out of his self-preoccupation. Looking back on his life on the mountain, he realized that it had been, yes, gemlike perhaps, as he'd seen it on the night they left. But it had also lacked what he now knew was a necessity. It was painful to face, but he no longer looked forward to returning to the mountain. He couldn't imagine being there without Sisul.

He thought, "What will become of me now? Sisul will find her family, as she must. I truly want her to. But I'll be alone again. Well Bruce, you've managed before. I guess you can do it again."

The origin of Wachussami goes back no one knows how many years, to the time when an Indian family or two decided to stop at a certain place below the tumbling falls in a river close to the sea. Perhaps these first settlers, Sisul Osborn's forebears, were hungry, and thought this a likely place for plentiful fish and game. Perhaps they were fugitives from a tribal war and sought safety there. Or maybe they had simply gotten tired of wherever it was they came from and found this place to their liking. They saw how the water churned into milk below the falls, gradually cleared and sparkled clean in the sunlight, then swept past a small island, where the wolves howled at night. Every spring salmon struggled up the river to spawn and moose tramped through the dark woods, their rutting-season bellows echoing across the valleys and down to the river's edge. Perhaps the fruits of the earth didn't grow easily there, but these people had never known ease. Centuries of survival had taught them how to find what the earth held, and the sea and river provided food in abundance — oysters and clams, shad and salmon, lobsters, alewives. In the woods were Gluskabe's gifts of hare and deer, bear and moose and caribou. Life was hard and short, but the Indians who settled here and in other parts of Maine considered it their promised land, a place especially created for the chosen people, the Wabanakis.

When the white man first arrived, he came only as a woodsman and a hunter, and Wachussami stayed much as it was. But around the turn of the century a mill had somehow sat itself down; Indian labor even helped build the thick brick walls. Its shadow cast the south side of the river in perpetual darkness, and now the river began to seem faintly malevolent. Machines turned night and day, drowning out the forest sounds, which had been as familiar a part of the old life as the air itself. And soon the air changed too, sucked up by the acrid fumes that poured out of the tall mill chimneys. Soon it was evident that spring would never again be signaled by the leap of salmon over the falls.

XVII

Bruce was remembering how, as a kid, he used to play a game in which somebody had to look for a hidden object. "Am I getting warm?" he would ask, and the others would say, "No, no, you're still cold, stone cold." Then suddenly everybody would shout, "You're getting warm now, warmer, warmer. Oh, you're hot, very hot!"

Now he felt that he and Sisul were getting warmer as they worked their way along Penobscot Bay, camping out in fog and rain or on wild nights when the stars crackled and surf blew up over the rocks.

"Ever hear of a place called Wachussami?" he always asked in stores where they bought their day's supply of groceries.

One morning an old lobsterman spoke up. "Down east about fifty miles, inland; a little village up the river a ways."

Bruce shot quick glances at Sisul on the night before they arrived in Wachussami and saw that she was preoccupied. He couldn't make up his mind whether to say anything.

"What do you think you'll find tomorrow?" he finally said quietly. "Please don't say, 'I don't know,' " he added.

It was a warm night; their small fire was burning out. Sisul studied the coals that were blinking like red eyes in the dark.

"Maybe . . . nothing," she said. "Or the same. Like you said. A five-and-ten, a garage."

"Did your mother ever tell you about it?"

"She said . . . it was home." Could she make Bruce understand what she meant by that word? "She said we would go back someday. It was where she grew up, her sisters and brother, her grandmother; where they hunted and fished together . . . It was Gluskabe's country, where he made the Indians come out of the ash trees; where his animals ran and raised their families. When my mother was little they would catch salmon when it came up the river, and later they'd go down to the sea and fish. All summer long, she said, there was a smell of smoke through the woods from the fires drying the fish. And in the fall there would be great hunts. The men would run off blowing on special horns made to sound like moose calls, and there would be a great feast, with deer and moose and pheasant to eat, and Indians would come from all over. The men would dress themselves up and dance, and the women, too . . .

"But my mother said she couldn't remember much; she was very little in those days. She said it changed and there was not so much to eat anymore, and her older sisters and brother went away and never came back. She was the youngest in her family and finally she went away too, and left her mother behind.

"Wachussami was a special place, my mother said. Magic happened there . . ."

Bruce nodded sadly. Which was more painful, he wondered. To have imagined a special place . . . magic . . . and to find that it no longer existed, or never to have had the chance to imagine such things at all?

"Do you think your grandmother is still alive?"

"Oh, no. She would be too old."

He got up and poured water on the coals, letting the steam rise and melt away each time before he poured on more water.

"Well, whatever happens, we'll work something out," he said, more to reassure himself than her.

Sisul didn't sleep well that night. Excitement,

fear, and strange feelings she could scarcely catch hold of were churning inside her. The later it got, the more her thoughts sank into half dreams; she began to hear and see her mother, who seemed to be standing at the entrance to a long dark tunnel that went back, back forever into a time so long ago that no one's mind could comprehend it, to a time when all of Maine, all of the land of the north, was wild, and filled only with cries of animals or now and then with an Indian voice calling out in a language no one understood anymore. Beyond this was a beautiful silence, a stillness that would never be again.

A poignant sense of loss woke Sisul up. As she lay there under her blankets she began to cry. For the first time since she had run away, a feeling of true loneliness and desolation came over her. It was not just her own loneliness she felt, but the loneliness of all the Indian people set to wander in this world that had once fit them so well.

Off the main road from the center of town there was a dirt road, almost a path, that led out to the river, down below the falls. Beside the path sat a one-room tarpaper shack, the home of Ashuket, the old Indian basket woman. Everybody in town knew her; she seemed as old and ageless as the rocks themselves.

Ashuket liked to keep the radio going while she shuffled around the cabin. She'd gotten up late this morning, and here was the noontime news on already. She put away the dishes from breakfast, her crippled hands not yet warmed up, still so stiff. It would be a while before she'd be able to cut more splints out of the ash; she'd have to sit in the sun first and let her old body get warm. Thank God or Gluskabe or the Great Being or Jesus or whoever it was you were supposed to thank for the sun and heat. Why He — whoever He was — couldn't be generous enough to let it be warm all year long was a question she had thought about off and on through her lifetime. It was probably because someone had been bad long ago — that was the excuse they always gave you when life got hard — but why she had to be punished along with the others she could never understand. *She* had never been bad — not *bad* bad, anyway; nothing anyone should get so upset about as to make the sun not shine for months at a time.

How many moons before hard winter set in again? Five or six at the most. She didn't see how she could live through another winter, not down here by the river, anyhow; it was too damp, and the wind came right up and blew through the walls, no matter how much paper she stuffed in, right through her skin, hitting her bones, making her so stiff she could hardly move. The winters always creaked by, too, and the summer sun, it was gone like tossing water over rocks.

Old Rudy — was it Rudy? She'd forgotten which of her three husbands it was — all dead, one of the coughing sickness, another in an accident at the mill, and Rudy, the last one, who was French-Canadian, he'd just gone of old age, the way she would soon.

She guessed it was old Rudy who used to say the harder a winter was the tougher it made you. People who lived farther south were soft, like oysters; no good to anybody. Rudy had been to those places — Boston, New York — he was a traveler, that man. How many nights had been whiled away listening to his stories? Maybe he made them all up. She sometimes thought he did, but it was true: the sports from down there looked the way he said, their faces soft and white, dressed in funny-looking things, the women's feet stuck into things on sticks; it was a queer way for anybody to want to walk. Not that she herself didn't like jewelry. Jewelry was her passion, and she always stared at the women who stopped, with their shiny bracelets and rings. Once a family stopped to see her baskets and a little dog jumped out of the car and — she could hardly believe her eyes — the dog had on a necklace that caught the flash of the sun as he ran around yipping and going on all her baby corn plants.

All her life she had picked up junk wherever she went and made something out of it to hang around her neck or wrists — shells, stones, broken glass, bits of tin cans. She collected cellophane cigarette wrappers and had a special way of folding and weaving them to make belts or bracelets; they were pretty, but didn't last too long. The only time she ever stole in her whole life was when the five-and-ten opened up in town and she saw the rings with red glass stones. She took one and for some reason didn't pay for it, though she'd had enough money with her. It was only that once; she'd never do it again. It was dangerous if they caught you stealing. Old Sebatis took up stealing and they caught him and put him away and he died there, some place called Thomaston, so far away from home. Anyway, the red glass soon fell out and got lost and she'd never been able to find it; it was probably down between the floorboards somewhere. White man's junk, you had to watch out. She'd heard of Indians selling land for a bit of stuff that fell apart a week later. She was too smart for that and kept away from the five-and-ten, though she did buy this radio from a man who came around selling it for only four dollars. That wasn't such a bad price, and the words and music were wonderful, the way they kept her company now she was alone.

Yes, she was smart, but not smart enough to move when they put the new road in. Now she was stuck out here by the river; no tourists ever came by to see her baskets, and even if she was 92 — some folks said she was 100, but she didn't see how she could be so old — her baskets were still better than Marie's. Marie had a combination basket shop and poolroom in town. She said she made $50 on baskets last summer, but maybe she was lying; you couldn't trust an Indian any more than you could an *awenotc* these days.

On nice days Ashuket would take as many baskets as she could carry and sit out by the crossroads. It was a good place because there was shade under the pine trees and it was the road into town from the south, so people saw her baskets first, before they got

172

to Marie's place. Sometimes they'd stop and look as if they were going to buy one, then go on. But later they'd come back, stop again, and buy hers. She figured they'd seen Marie's and decided hers were better. Cheaper, too. More often, though, they'd drive right past and she'd see them come out again later. Sitting on the back shelf of the car would be a basket or two. It made her mad because she knew her work was better.

What was that? A shadow at the door, somebody here to buy a basket, they must have heard about her . . .

"Yeah?" she called out and shuffled over to the screen door. "You want baskets?" She squinted into the sunlight and felt with her fingers to see that her blouse was buttoned, then smoothed out her long skirt. "Wait while I turn down the radio," she said, shuffling back into the dark.

"Sure, we'll buy a few," Bruce called in and took out his wallet. Sisul stood beside him and peered into the shack, from which came a pungent smell of dried fish.

"We wanted to talk a little too, if you've got the time," Bruce said as the old lady emerged from the dark.

"Talk, oh yes, fine," she said and pushed the door open. "Sit in the sun," she said, stepping uncertainly off the big stone that served as a doorstep. She settled herself on an old kitchen chair at the side of the house. "You sit there." She pointed to some crates that had baskets in various stages of manufacture piled on them. "Take that stuff off," she said.

"She's so old," Sisul thought. "She doesn't see very well."

"This girl," Bruce said, pointing to Sisul, "is Wabanaki. Her name is Sisul Osborn; her mother's name was Awatawessu Denis. Her mother married a white man named Osborn. We're trying to find out if she has any family around here. Can you tell us anything?"

"Oh, sure," Ashuket said, leaning back and letting the sun hit her face. "Sure, I help you." Her eyes closed and she saw the colors that play in front of the eyes when you look into bright sun. It was always a wonder to her how that happened; she liked it ... A girl went off with a white man; such an old story! Which one, she wondered; which one was this girl's mother?

She opened her eyes a crack and peered at the girl. She was Wabanaki, all right, but that was no Indian nose. She'd kept the color. Some of them looked so pasty. What kind of story to tell them? She could make it up; it was all the same anyway: a good-looking white fellow came around, fooled with you, teased, bought you things, gave you money. Hadn't it happened to her, too? Except she had never gone off with one, something always made her stay here, maybe it was a mistake. There wasn't anything to make up, really. Osborn, Osborn ... no, it could be Smith, Jones, Brown, Osborn — what difference did it make?

174

"She ran off with some fellow. She's gone; they all gone now," she said out loud.

"Can you tell us something about her?" Bruce asked. It looked as if she was falling asleep. A fly had settled on her hand.

"Sure, I tell you the story," she said. Her eyes were closed, but she waved away the fly, a sign of life. "How many baskets you buy?"

"Is five enough?" Bruce took out his wallet again.

"Okay, sure, five plenty." She didn't take any notice of the wallet. "First I tell you a story," she said. She paused. Did she have the strength to go through it all this morning, she wondered. Yes, but five baskets; that could be as much as a dollar. Besides, once she got started the strength would come to her. It always did, she mustn't think about it so much, just start and the rest would follow, like a little brook running to a stream, the stream running into river, river into ocean, ocean into sky ... it would all follow ...

"Once there was a big Wabanaki family named Denis, also Mitchell. But this girl's family was Denis. They were the Bears, or Wanderers; many chiefs come from this family. Now I'll tell you the story of the Bears."

She settled back, her closed eyes dark slits cut deep across the web of wrinkles, an old woman droning in the sun.

"Many lives ago there was a man, a wilderness house man; his clothing was sheets of moss, and his belt was twigs such as men wore then. He and his

175

squaw and boy left the village; they go way north to a big council and dance. Up the river they went and far along, far along. After many looks, they have to make a carry. The man goes ahead with the canoe on his back, the woman carries goods, and the boy runs alongside, as was the custom. The wife is busy, too slow, and the boy is so full of jumping he runs ahead to be with the father. But the little boy gets lost, his father went on too fast. When squaw and father join they see what has happened. They search over the land, but do not find him. They go back to the village and many moons pass while all the men of the village go to hunt for the boy.

"When the snow melts some hunters see sharpened sticks near water and say, 'Ah, we see the boy is still alive and catching fish!' And they see footprints of bears laying all about. They run home and tell the father, 'Your son has become a son of bears!'

"Now there is a lazy man in the village. He never took part in the hunting for the boy. But *now* he goes out to the bear's den and knocks with his bow on the rocks lying there. This knocking makes a great noise inside the den. First the father bear, then the mother, and then the baby bear go to the opening of the den and every time the lazy man kills them. He goes into the cave and sees the little boy, who is afraid and sitting in the dark corner all in a ball. So the lazy man carries him home and gets a big reward; he is a big man now. But the little boy is turning into a bear! Already bristles are showing on his back and shoulders and his ways changed. He is afraid of his father and other people."

Ashuket opened her eyes to see if they were listening. Yes, they were still interested; she would go on.

"But it came out all right. After only one moon they got him back into a person again and when he grew up he was a strong Indian man. He got married and had children, and all these children and their children through many lives were called Bears. And wherever they went they always drew a picture of a bear on a piece of birch bark and left it at their camps. They always drew bears on all their belongings to mean, 'I am one of the Bears. My father was one, and my father's father, and on and on.' They are big people. Many chiefs were Bears."

Sisul had been listening and if she closed her eyes could almost believe she was hearing her mother's voice. The story wasn't new to her. She had heard it many times; could almost have recited it along with the old woman, and in the same words.

"Is this a Bear's knife?" Sisul asked, holding out her mother's knife so that the old woman could see the carvings on the handle.

The old woman blinked her eyes open and studied the knife. "Yes," she said, turning it over in her knotted fingers. "You are a Bear and your mother was a Bear. Your name was Denis; all Denis are Bears."

"And you really knew my mother?" Sisul asked.

The old lady bent toward her to return the knife,

and for a moment looked deep into Sisul's eyes. "How can I lie to this girl?" That thought flared up in her old brain. "She is one of us, she is like me, I ought not. But the baskets," she thought.

"Which baskets you want?" she said, pointing toward the rope at the corner of the shack from which the finished baskets hung. "You go choose the baskets you like while I think here. Your father's name — what did you say?"

"Osborn." Bruce shouted to make sure she heard him. "Len Osborn." He handed her a five-dollar bill; then went off with Sisul to get the baskets.

Ashuket looked at the money, turning it over and over in her hands. When they came back she stuffed it in the pocket of her skirt.

"You pay me too much," she said. She sounded almost angry.

"I know," Bruce said.

"When somebody pays so much it's because he wants a true story or he wants a good story. Which one you want?"

"What do you think?" Bruce asked.

"I guess . . . the truth," she said, and sighed.

"That's right," Bruce said, looking at Sisul, whose face was now solemn.

"Yes, you could say I know your mother. I know her, she is a Bear, she ran off with a lumberman. He was a nice man, very happy, smiling all the time, and he made her happy, so she went away with him."

"Sisul had a grandmother left behind. Did you know her?"

178

"You must listen to what I say." The old woman opened her eyes for a second. "I said, 'You could say I knew your mother . . .' but you could also say I didn't. So many, so many . . . I live so long, so many go, all up and down the river, and those who not go off, those who stay here, most die, everybody die, that one winter very bad . . ."

Suddenly the old woman seemed to wake up. She sat forward and opened her eyes.

"You are the daughter of those two, a Bear and a lumberman?" She looked hard at Sisul.

"Well, then, you could say — oh, I don't know — I was married to a Bear once, long, long ago. I might be your great-aunt. I hardly remember him, it was so long. There was a sister, hardly more than a girl then; she had a baby girl and used to carry her around the old way in a papoose while she went fishing for bass in this river here. Maybe that was your grandmother, I don't know. Fish are gone now, no more. River farther up, it's not so bad, still some trout. Here, nothing, all yellow and smells bad."

Bruce interrrupted. "Were there any more relatives? Does Sisul have an aunt or uncle, a cousin?"

"Oh, I don't know, maybe a sister come back. I remember something like that. Long time ago, she probably dead too now. Maybe in another town you find somebody, up the river, they all along the river here, many Indians, some Denis, I don't know how many, so many die, go away . . ."

"The sister — what was her name?"

The old woman laughed. "You think I remember

179

so many names? She was a Denis, a Bear, you ask around, somebody know what happened to her. Ask Marie, she know, in town, the poolhall . . ."

Slowly she got off the chair and went over to Sisul, lifted up her face and looked into it.

"Yes, you that girl's granddaughter, it might be. You have the eyes, big, pointed at corner. Funny nose, though. What happened to your mother?"

"She died too," Sisul said, turning her face away. "She had the coughing sickness too."

"Well, here is something for you," Ashuket said, and took off the necklace of teeth she was wearing. "Maybe some of these bear teeth." She laughed, and put the necklace over Sisul's head. Then she turned and started to go inside.

"I very tired these days," she said. "Very tired and have no more story to tell. The story is always sad. If you buy a basket, put the money under the door." She went up the porch step; the screen door flapped shut behind her.

Sisul was about to call out that they had already bought five baskets, but Bruce put his hand up to her mouth. He took out his wallet for the third time, and shoved a ten-dollar bill into one of the tears in the screen.

"Should I leave more?" he whispered, still holding the wallet.

"How much have you got left?"

"Sixty."

"Better not," Sisul said with a sigh.

XVIII

They were gathering up their things when Ashuket came flopping out the door again, this time chewing on some tobacco. It was as if she had forgotten they were going to leave, and now they were old friends to her, neighbors even, expected there. She took her knife out of her pocket and began work on a basket.

"You know," she said, "I think, oh by golly, you best come fast, Gluskabe, you come fast. But now I see he not coming this time; maybe later, after I'm gone. Maybe when you an old lady like me" — she looked up at Sisul, smiling — "maybe then Gluskabe come and change all this back."

She leaned back, let the sun beat down on her brown wrinkled skin, and lifted her arm and waved her old hand across, as if to touch the tree tops.

"Once this all forest, with bear and mink and otter, beaver, too, all, all forest, and cold water, with salmon and shad and bass and trout. Many, many trout. This all come back.

"See that stone there?" She pointed with her foot to a flat, round stone that was sitting behind the cabin, looking out over the river.

"That my stone — that me," she exclaimed, and laughed. "You take that stone, go on, take it, and you lift it up and throw it, crash it down, it never break. It's good stone, a good hard stone. Some stones like that, others no good, they smash up when you crash them, but not that one. That my stone. When I die, I go into that stone. That's what Gluskabe tells me. One night he says, 'Ashuket, you are a stone, no matter how you're bounced and crashed, you such a good stone you always stay the same.' So the next morning I look for the stone, and sure enough, there it was, sitting right there where it is, and I picked it up and crashed it and it didn't break, it didn't get even a scratch, so I knew that was me, that was what Gluskabe meant.

"And I believe he sent you here for me to tell you this, because when I die I want you to take that stone, lift it up, and carry it with you wherever you

182

go. That will be me, with you always! And because I'm heavy, you won't be able to go very far." She laughed again.

"You won't be able to wander away so easy, like your mother, not with that stone along, oh no!

"You promise me now, that's what you'll do? You take that stone, and you'll know I'm in there, and you'll keep it with you, and sometimes you'll talk to me, eh, say, 'Hey, Ashuket, how are you, what's it like in there? You warm enough?' Things like that sometimes, just to let me know you think of me. Promise me you do that?"

"I promise," Sisul said. "I promise."

"What about you?" she said, turning to Bruce. "You going to keep this girl?"

"Why . . ." Bruce spluttered.

"You not her father." She paused, waiting for his answer.

"No, I'm not her father."

"You not her brother, either."

"No."

"You not her husband."

"No."

"You not her sweetheart."

"No."

"Then what are you? Why you stay with her?"

Bruce was silent a long time. Finally he said, "No, I'm not any of those things. But I care for her. She's the only person I ever cared for."

He could feel Sisul staring at him.

"You got nobody else? No wife or child?"

"No."

"Well, then, I guess you need this girl. She help you on the boat?"

"Boat? You misunderstand . . ."

"Why you not help him?" she scolded Sisul. "A lobsterman needs help; it's hard work, out at morning so early it's still night, cold and wet. You be good help to him, or else I not give you my stone."

Bruce and Sisul exchanged looks and smiled.

"Okay, that's okay," Ashuket said, nodding her head. "Now," she said, "you go because I very tired. Then you come back sometime and one day when you come and when you see I am dead, you take the stone. You blow on the stone, that way I'll know it's you, maybe put your cheek next to it, warm me up a little. Okay, you promise?"

XIX

It happened so quickly. They had gone to Marie's poolhall, learned from Marie that Sisul's aunt, Sinshussi, had returned to Wachussami some years ago and was now living near the edge of town. They hardly knew what to say to each other as they walked along the quiet country road: sometimes words are like quicksand, pulling you down into some new awareness from which there's no going back. And so you don't speak.

The house sat by itself at the side of the road in a scrubby, flat place. Nothing much grew there; the soil was sandy, full of rocks. Farther down the road on the left was a Coca-Cola sign, and beyond that glimmered a patch of blue sea.

Her heart pounding, Sisul hastened up the sagging porch steps. Bruce followed and knocked softly on the screen door.

"Come in," someone called out.

Silhouetted in the dim afternoon sun was the deeply grained face of an Indian woman. She sat in an upholstered chair, her hands extended to the edges of its arms, a tattered quilt draped around her shoulders. Aside from the chair, the house was furnished with a kitchen table and chair, a gas stove, and, over by the window, an iron cot. Resting on the table was a single can of condensed milk.

Sisul stood by the door. "I am Sisul. My mother was Awatawessu, Awatawessu Denis." Her voice sounded loud in the still room.

"This is not your father," the woman said. These first words were almost inaudible, as if they were emerging from some deep hollow place.

"No. My father is dead. So is Awatawessu, my mother."

No emotion passed across the time-worn face; no muscle moved.

"This man brought you here?"

"Yes."

Sometimes more is said by silence than a rush of words. All three people in the room felt the silence throbbing around them; it was almost something they could touch.

"Why did you not stay with your father's people?"

Alarm flashed through Sisul's breast. "Why does she ask that?" she protested to herself. "Isn't it good that I'm here?" Aloud she said, "I . . . they didn't want me. I didn't want to stay."

"But that is why my sister took you there. To stay with them."

"Not to stay there!"

"She had the sickness. She said they would raise you like a white girl; they were rich and would take care of you."

For Bruce to look at Sisul's face was punishment. He stared out the window.

"They didn't," Sisul said at last.

"They weren't good to her," Bruce blurted out, turning back. "From what I can figure out it was pretty damned bad there. Sisul ran away when her mother died. This girl lived by herself in a cave all winter. That's where I found her, like a wild animal."

Sinshussi made no reply. The room had grown darker. It was going to rain soon. There seemed to be nothing more to say: everything and nothing had already been said.

"Do you go to school?" she finally asked.

"No."

"What is your age now?"

"I'm almost thirteen."

"You know I am Sinshussi, your mother's sister."

Sisul was suddenly reminded of the female deer with whom she had exchanged looks across the winter snowbank. The doe had seemed to say, "No, you cannot share anything with me." If Sisul's own dark eyes could have spoken, they would have said, "Please let me in. You are all I have."

Still there was silence in the room. No one breathed. Bruce couldn't bear to watch or listen anymore. He quietly let himself out the door and sat down on the porch steps.

As he left, Sinshussi spoke. "Metcigak nla-bin elaba-zim-uk. Da-li-naga-lana ... Do you know that?"

"No, aunt, I don't know those words."

"Your mother should have taught you. They are from the Song of the Deserted Woman. What of our songs do you know?"

Sisul wanted to explain how her mother had been afraid to let her be — how to say it — too Indian. The Osborns wouldn't have liked it. But she understood that she couldn't say such a thing to this woman. "Not many," she answered. "I know some songs — a lullaby ..."

Why won't she ask me to sit down, Sisul wondered. Why does she keep me standing here?

"So you did not go to white school," Sinshussi said.

"No. Mother needed me to help her."

"But you are not Indian, either. She did not teach you Indian ways."

"Oh, yes! She showed me how to find food, how to

live by myself; she told me all about Gluskabe . . ."

Sinshussi interrupted. "But you cannot speak our language." Her voice began to rise, for the first time losing its remoteness. "All that other — is nothing. Look at the way you hold yourself, the way you talk! The way you walk into my house with that man. I can see. Ten years with white people. You are . . ." She whispered the words, as if they were too ugly to say out loud — "a half-breed."

Sisul put her hands over her ears and tried to shut out the sound, but her aunt's voice droned relentlessly on.

"I said to your mother when she began fooling with that lumberman that it would end up bad, that she could not stay Wabanaki and go live in his house. She couldn't ever be white, no matter how he dressed her up or gave her a fancy place to live in. But she never listened. She was bewitched by him; she could never see anything but him.

"Now see what happens! She is dead and nobody wants you. Why should they? You are nothing, a bird without wings, a deer without legs. You come here with that *awenotc*. One day you'll put more half-breeds in the world. Go on. Why did you come here?"

Through glistening tears Sisul watched Sinshussi turn her face away and stare at the wall. For a brief moment she wanted to run to the chair, fall on her knees, and plead to be listened to, to be understood. "You are all I have," she cried out to herself.

But, she realized, you couldn't beg for what should

be given freely. You couldn't make somebody want you.

She turned and started out the door.

"Wait." The old woman spoke. "If you have no place else to go, you can stay here. Do you have money? I cannot feed you."

Sisul did not allow herself to look back. As she went out the door she said only, "No, I have nothing."

Bruce was waiting for her on the porch steps. Without speaking, they walked a few yards from the house, then sat down at the side of the road. A few days ago Sisul would have wanted to run off to be alone to cry. Oh yes, she could make the tears come now if she wanted to. But what good would they do? Tears were a solace, and there was no solace for her loss. As for wanting to be alone — well, that was of no use either. She could not be alone now. She had Bruce to consider.

Sisul looked up at Bruce and saw his concern. "She offered to let me stay," she said.

"Do you want to?" Bruce asked. Waiting for her answer would be one of the hardest things he would ever have to do.

Up to now, Sisul saw, she had believed that Indians were superior beings, half gods. Once she met with them, she'd thought, they would reach out and take her into their special world. Then she would never have had to plan or worry again. By itself, her life would have found its natural pattern. How foolish, how childish that had been! Indians were hu-

190

man, not gods. They were poor and sick, pushed aside by a new world.

"No," she finally answered. "I don't *want* to. But at least it's a place to stay until I can find something better. Maybe Marie could use me to help make baskets . . ."

"I only asked if you *want* to. You said no. So that's that. Come on, let's go." Bruce pulled himself off the ground.

Sisul remained seated. "I can't go back to the mountain. Walter would find me in no time, and I won't go back to the Osborns. Staying here's the best I can do."

Bruce reached down, grasped her hand, and pulled her up. "No, we can find something better. I'm sure we can. Let's have something to eat while we think about it."

XX

Bruce was busy cutting slices of Selgie's cheese. "I wish I knew what to say."

Sisul didn't know what to say, either. She couldn't even raise her eyes to look at Bruce.

"When I was a kid I thought men my age had all the answers. But they don't. At least *I* don't . . . Can you tell me what you're thinking?"

"I'm looking for a Wabanaki answer to things," she said slowly.

"Go on," Bruce murmured.

"The basket lady keeps coming into my head. She made me sad. Mad, too."

Bruce was perplexed. "What would make you get mad at that old lady?"

"I guess the way things were when we got there. The radio going, her place looking so messy. And how she kept asking you to buy baskets. I ... I wanted to be proud of her. I couldn't."

It surprised Bruce to hear this. "It's not her fault she's old, that she has to sell baskets."

"I know ..."

"I should think if you were going to be mad at anybody it would be your aunt."

Sisul shook her head. "I understand what she did. She's trying to keep the old ways. That's what she wanted my mother to do."

"But your mother tried, Sisul. Look at all she taught you. I don't think your aunt could understand how hard it was."

Sisul was fingering the beads Ashuket had given her.

"I'm glad Ashuket told us about the Bears," Bruce said. "I bet she knows lots more stories. You want to see her again?"

Sisul shrugged. "I can make it out there by myself if I want to."

"You don't understand," Bruce said. "I'd like to go. I liked her."

Both of them were preoccupied with thoughts about the future as they walked out to Ashuket's shack. When they got there a small group of Indians was gathering. It was quietly explained what had happened.

Ashuket had gone out in the afternoon, as she usually did, to sit surrounded by her baskets at the side of the road. Someone passing by noticed her there, unchanged from when he'd gone by a few hours before.

"Her body gave up to time," an old woman said solemnly. "Now her spirit is going across the star road."

Marie was there, sitting on the stone step. "She's probably making her baskets up there," she murmured. "Nothing can make her stop." Marie went on to tell Bruce and Sisul that it had been decided to bury Ashuket in the old way. Some of the men had gone ahead to get the *buskanigan* — the birch bark — ready. People were gathering now to go join them at the burial place.

Bruce suggested moving on, feeling he might not be wanted.

"Walking over here," Sisul said, "I kept thinking, 'If I say good-by to Ashuket maybe it'll help me say good-by to my dreams about Wachussami, too.'"

"You've got to do that, haven't you," Bruce said.

She nodded, then grabbed his hand. "Let's go with them. Afterward we'll come back to get her stone."

Bruce looked puzzled for a moment. "Oh sure, I remember now. That stone she wanted you to keep."

As they followed the others up the switch-backed path to a bluff above the river they began to hear voices echoing through the woods. A plaintive chant was being repeated over and over. Men had formed a circle around the laid-out figure of Ashuket. Now the others quietly joined them.

Ashuket was dressed in her best clothes with all her jewelry hung around her neck and wrists. The singing softly died away as a few of the old men placed her body in the roll of birch bark, the *buskanigan*. It was lowered into the ground.

The oldest man, his voice breaking with emotion, began to chant again, and this time Sisul and Bruce joined in, saying the sounds with the others:

ya ni go we ya ni go we ya   we go we

The melody carried even Bruce and Sisul into the mood that all now shared — a mood of regret for time past — along with a special sense of chosenness for having shared in that time.

As the group moved down the bluff toward the old river that had witnessed so much, the sun cast its last orange light over the horizon. Everyone quietly wished each other farewell.

Walking along the riverbank path with Sisul, Bruce smiled bitterly for all the thoughts he used to have about wanting to die alone in the distant north. Now he felt an overwhelming need to be part of this world around him, to share in its sadnesses and rejoicings, as well as its failings.

Early stars began to come out above the tree tops. "This night is special," Sisul thought. It surprised her, but she was no longer sad. Funerals were supposed to be sad. She had many other reasons to be sad, too. But she had taken part in an old Wabanaki custom on the bluff. She began to feel a deep happiness. "The old ways do go on," she thought.

The Milky Way banded the sky over Ashuket's shack. Sisul went to the stone and sat beside it. "The Star Road — what you call the Milky Way. What is it, really?" she asked Bruce.

"A lot of stars. Millions, I guess."

"You could say — they're like lit-up steppingstones across the sky."

"Steppingstones to where?"

"To where everybody's spirit goes. Oh, I know it's not really so. But it's nice to think that Gluskabe's out there. And now Ashuket. My mother's name, Awatawessu, means 'star.' She could be one of those little pieces of light."

"Maybe," Bruce murmured. "What's hard to believe is that even though those stars look as if they're right next to each other, like the pebbles down in our stream — or steppingstones, as you said — they're really far apart. Millions and millions of miles, maybe."

Sisul said thoughtfully, "Then that would mean each one of them would have to be — well, maybe not all alone, because they could see each other. Just as we can see them. But independent. Is that the right word?"

"Yes. Independent. That's a good word."

"Together, but still independent."

Moments of silence passed; then Sisul added, "Strong, too. You have to be strong to be by yourself."

"Maybe it's better not to be so strong," Bruce murmured to himself.

"Sisul," he asked, "how'd you like to go live on an island? We can do some asking around, see what's possible. I saw a place called Isle au Haut on the map. It looks high; it's got a lot of space; there are fishing villages ... Maybe" — he peered at her through the dark — "even a school. Ashuket said I ought to be a lobsterman. You want to help me, like she said?"

Sisul remained seated by Ashuket's stone, looking at the stars.

"Well, what do you think?" Bruce persisted. "Shall we give it a try?"

"What do you mean? Try what?"

"Try living on that island. Haven't you been listening?"

"How long would it take you to get me there? You have to get back to the mountain soon. It'll be too late to get your garden started if you don't."

"Sisul," Bruce said solemnly, "I mean to stay with you. We'll go together and I'll stay with you as long as you want me to."

197

"No, no," she protested. "The mountain is where you want to be. I'll get along."

"Listen, Sisul, I've come to feel that those years up there — well, they're over now. I can't go back. It has nothing to do with you. Don't think I'm giving something up because of you. It's just the opposite."

She shook her head. "You *belong* there. It's the right place for you."

"A lonely mountain isn't enough, Sisul."

"It's *not* lonely. It's your home."

"It seems lonely now. I tell you, I can't go back."

"You're just saying that. Bruce, long ago I promised I wouldn't bother you. I haven't lived up to that. Let me do it now."

"Okay."

"Then you'll go back?" she asked.

"No, I'm staying with you. Nothing would bother me more than leaving you behind."

Afterword

Some years later two figures were observed strolling along the beach after a storm. They were looking over the debris — shells, orange peels, driftwood, rocks — that had been washed up on shore.

A stranger watching them thought to himself, "Wonder why that old lobsterman isn't working to-day? Too rough for him out there, maybe. Now that's a funny thing! What's he picking up that big rock for and giving it to that Indian woman? What's he think she's going to do with it? Bet she'll throw it away as soon as his back is turned."

The stranger moved on, so he never learned the destination of the rock. Only if he'd been more curious would he have heard the lobsterman's voice blowing across the wind and surf: "Here it is. You can call it my stone. Put it next to Ashuket's. Talk to it once in a while, as you do to hers. Let it sit in the sun and rain. And if it cracks and breaks apart someday, well, I guess that's all right, too. And someday — promise me — you've got to get a stone for yourself. Make sure you find somebody who'll care for it."

"I promised Ashuket," Sisul answered. "Now I promise for your stone. I'll try for my own, too. But right now," she said with a laugh, "I've got to leave the stone right here." She put it down at the entrance of the path to her cabin. "My muscles ache from hauling in those lobster pots yesterday. I'm still not as strong as you are."

Bruce was about to turn toward his own place when Sisul said, "Can't you come in for a moment? I want to show you something." Her eyes were shining, just as they always had. But her body had finally grown to match her head. No one would think to call her pumpkin head anymore.

Bruce sat down in Sisul's one chair while she put on a kettle of water. He really wanted to go to his cabin, where he could stretch out and ease the pain he was feeling. He thought back to those hard days when he'd been making the dam. How had he ever done it!

"Here," Sisul said, shyly, handing him a sheaf of papers. "They're all there; every myth I can remember. Can you read my writing?"

Despite his fatigue, Bruce was deeply moved. He knew she'd been working to get the myths written down for several years now, grabbing every moment she could after a hard day's work out in the bay.

She waited nervously as he looked through the folder of papers. As he read he began to get more and more drawn in. Sometimes he laughed out loud. "You never told me this one about the rabbit tying a bone on his forehead. They're wonderful, Sisul."

He read on. "I can almost see that silly rabbit trying to climb a tree and act like a woodpecker! Can I take these with me? I want to read them again when I'm not so tired."

Sisul's eyes blazed with pride.

"As for that stone," Bruce said, "forget it. I wasn't all that serious."

But the time did come, and sooner than Sisul had dared let herself imagine that day, when she found herself going out to the special cove she'd chosen for Ashuket's stone. There she placed Bruce's stone. She knelt beside it, put her arms over it, and cried.

It was a silly delusion, this stone business. Over the years she and Bruce had discussed it and sometimes laughed a little over it. "I guess we'll have to drag that damned stone around with us wherever we go," he used to say about Ashuket's stone.

"Yet," he said once, "I can see that it's good to have something you can touch that keeps you in contact with a life that's meant something special to you. Sure, I know people who've been close to each other don't really need something so — so tangible —" He looked at Sisul to see if she understood that word, but he guessed she did because she was nodding her head in agreement.

"I visit Ashuket's stone sometimes," Sisul said. "Not because I have to. But I like to. I like to let my thoughts go into the stone. It carries me out to the Wabanaki world.

"Oh, I know Ashuket's spirit isn't really *in* that stone. It's just a piece of the earth. But the earth has seen everything."

"In some way," Bruce said, "I think Ashuket *is* in that stone. She was about as close as any person could ever get to the kind of endurance that's in good hard rock."

Now as she sat by the stones, remembering that conversation, Sisul thought about Bruce's use of the word *endurance*. "You had endurance too, Bruce," she said, as if he could hear her. "You'll always endure for me. Before you there'd been my mother. She gave me everything I learned about Wabanaki life. But I had to find a life for myself, too. Seeing how you changed, how you learned to like a new part of yourself — that meant a whole lot. And Bruce —" she reached over and touched the stone, "I promise you, I'll look hard to find someone to give my stone to."

Throughout this imaginary conversation it felt good to know she'd as much as told Bruce these things when he was alive. She was glad to know that when Bruce had died nothing had been left unsaid.

Once Bruce had complained that she was too grateful for what they'd done together. "I should have forced you into your generation's world. I should've made you go to school, meet people your own age. What do you have now?"

"For one thing, there isn't much I don't know about lobstering."

Bruce laughed. "That's true. All the mistakes I made, you made right along with me."

"You taught me how to read and write. You did it so well we take it for granted. Don't say you haven't done anything for me. When it comes to that, what did I ever do for you? You had to leave the mountain. Don't you wish you were back there sometimes?"

"Sometimes, I confess. In some ways it still seems a beautiful dream. But you can't live a dream, Sisul. I needed more than what that mountain was providing. These last years on the island have been the happiest of my life."

Sisul pulled herself away from the stones and stood watching the sea. "That's funny," she thought. "For the first time in years I just thought of myself as Aves. I've missed the mountain, too — my Aves existence."

It was time now to get back to her cabin and finish the project she and Bruce had been working on when he was ill. He'd enjoyed having the myths read to him, and as she did so, he'd occasionally interrupt and make suggestions about some way she might improve a sentence or change a word. She'd hurriedly scrawled notes, and now she wanted to get home and make all those corrections.

That was another way to keep in touch with Bruce, she thought. "A better way than weeping over that stone," she murmured to herself. "I know you wouldn't have wanted me to do *that*."

As she walked down the path through the woods, a smile brightened her face. She was remembering what Bruce had said one day after she'd read to him. "That old Gluskabe. You suppose he'll at least wave to me? I've gotten to feel pretty close to him. We both like pipes, too. That ought to help get a friendship started."